THE NINE LIVES OF JENNY CRUMB

Martina Dalton

WRITE AS RAIN BOOKS

Cover Design by Martina Dalton
Cover Model, Madeline Dalton
Photo by Tammy Davison

First Edition, 2015
ISBN 978-0-9897221-4-8

Dedication

This book is dedicated to Youth Theatre Northwest, the exceptional staff, and the many talented students they serve.

With love to Manny, Mimi, Jessi, Kate, Brian, Leslie, Stephanie, and John and Ellen Hill.

Acknowledgements

There are so many people to thank for making this novel possible.

First of all, I'd like to thank the staff, directors, stage managers, board, and everyone who has had a position at Youth Theatre Northwest for making the theatre such a special place for the thousands of kids who have called it a second home over the last thirty-two years. If you've ever worked at Youth Theatre Northwest, I'm talking to you. Thank you!

Special thanks to John and Ellen Hill for their dedication in keeping this gem of a theatre alive—and for their continuing efforts to build a new arts center (Mercer Island Center for the Arts—also known as MICA) which includes theatre, dance, music, and visual arts. Youth Theatre Northwest will find its permanent home there.

As always, many thanks to my critique group, Writers in the Rain (Fabio Bueno, Suma Subramaniam, Eileen Riccio, Brenda Beem, and Angela O. Peart) for their invaluable feedback and help with this novel.

Thank you to my wonderful editor, Alyssa Palmer, who is a wizard with words and who completes her editing passes with warp speed.

My family always deserves a round of applause for putting up with my weekly absences for my writing critique meetings, and for being supportive of my creative endeavors.

Thanks also to the real psychics, Pamela Jensen and Char Sundust. Their input helped to make my characters come alive.

To learn more about Youth Theatre Northwest: http://www.youththeatre.org/. And to learn more about MICA: http://www.mercerislandarts.org/.

Chapter 1

"The last time we were on a boat," Benny said with a twinkle in his eye, "an angel took a bullet for me."

I breathed in the last vestiges of summer and sighed. The water on Lake Washington was smooth as glass. An osprey swooped down from a tall fir tree and snatched a fish out of the water.

"The whole experience was so surreal." I focused my attention back to Benny. "The Tlingit warrior spirits and all of our totem animals banding together with the angels to protect us. Pretty cool."

Frank joined us on deck. "Are you kids enjoying the boat ride?"

Benny glanced at Frank and nodded. "We were just comparing it to our last boat ride up in Alaska."

"That was quite a trip." Frank handed us each a cold bottle of water. "It's hot out here. Do you want to get out of the sun?"

"Nah." Benny uncapped his bottle and took a sip. "School starts tomorrow. I want to enjoy every ray I can."

I eyed the pink on his arms. "You're burning. Might want to put some sunscreen on."

Benny pressed his finger to his arm and let go. A white fingerprint remained indented in his skin. "Hmph! So much for being a tanned god at school tomorrow."

"More like a pink diva," I joked.

"Hey!" He tried giving me an indignant look, but couldn't hold it. He burst out laughing. "I'm trying to be cool here."

1

"That's right." I dug through my tote bag, pulled out some lotion, and handed it to him. "You *are* going to be cool this year." I eyed his less-than-flattering shorts. "I'm taking you shopping at the mall tonight."

Benny squeezed some sunscreen onto his palm, rubbed his hands together, and spread it over his arms. "What look do you think I should go for? Preppy or hipster?"

"Hipster, definitely."

"Really? 'Cause I think I could rock the Izod polos and cable knit sweaters."

"Uh. No."

"All right. But if I get the crap beaten out of me, I'm holding you responsible."

"You'd be more likely to get the crap beaten out of you if you wore polos and cable knit sweaters."

"Okay, you two. You're starting to act like brother and sister. How 'bout if we go around the point here and take a look at Bill Gates' house?"

I gazed out at the shoreline. "Sure. Why not?"

Frank went back into the cabin and steered toward the McMansions nestled at the lake's edge. The glassy water reflected the subtle hues of the houses and flowering trees of the rich and famous.

We oohed and awed at the giant houses as we floated by.

Benny glanced at me and cleared his throat. "Have you talked to Ty or Cassandra lately?"

"Sort of. I've been texting them both. Ty seems pretty preoccupied, though. Sometimes days go by before I get a response."

"I thought he was really into you," Benny said.

"I think he was. But he's just hurting right now over the loss of his cousin. He kind of called off our relationship."

"He did?"

"Well, in a manner of speaking. He didn't say, 'I'm breaking up with you.' But he apologized and said he needed time to grieve and take care of his family. It's okay. I really like him, but…"

"But you're still hung up on Mike, right?"

A twinge of guilt washed over me. I was still angry with Mike for breaking up with me—just because his dad thought that having a girlfriend in his freshman year of college would be too distracting. Yet, I still really cared about him. That kind of attraction was something I'd never felt before.

"You're mad at yourself for still liking him."

"Benny, sometimes I hate that you're psychic." I blushed.

"I could say the same about you." He turned his attention back to the shoreline. "Is that it?"

A sprawling mansion was laid out on the lake's edge. It looked like a lodge that someone had stretched horizontally, like a piece of taffy.

Frank came back out on deck. "Well, what do you think?"

"That'll be mine someday," Benny said wistfully.

Frank lightly punched him on the arm. "You know, kid, I wouldn't be surprised if it was."

Good old Frank. He was almost like a grandfather to Benny and me. We had met him during the summer when we'd attended a psychic workshop with Celine. Thank God I had them both, because without them, I wouldn't have been able to find a missing boy—Devon. And by a twist of fate or perhaps divine intervention, Devon had turned out to be Frank's real grandson.

The three of us, along with Ty, Cassandra, and Detective Coalfield, had also managed to find Ty's missing cousin, River. Unfortunately, we found only her body. Her father had killed her, and had attempted to kill her mother for the insurance money.

"Ready to head back?" Frank glanced at his watch. "I'm taking Devon and my daughter out for pizza and a movie tonight." He chuckled. "My little grandson sure knows how to wrap his old grandpappy around his little finger. I'd do just about anything for that kid."

"Yeah," I answered. "He's got to make up for lost time. It's so nice that you've all reunited. But, you're right. We need to get going too. Benny is desperate for a makeover. That could take hours."

Chapter 2

I felt a thrill of excitement when we reached the school parking lot. Hard to believe this was the first day of my senior year in high school.

The sky was a cloudless blue. The temperature had already reached into the upper sixties, and it wasn't even seven-thirty in the morning yet.

Benny sat next to me in the passenger seat. He pushed his new black-framed glasses up on the bridge of his nose. The lenses had been popped out since Benny didn't actually *need* glasses.

"How do I look?"

I took in his outfit. Blues Brothers-style hat, white t-shirt, and jeans rolled at the cuff. He was anxiously rubbing the strap of his tan leather messenger bag lying across his lap.

"You look good, Benny."

"Good? Just good?" He looked panic-stricken. "Oh my God, maybe I should've bought the green Izod sweater. I knew I should've gone for preppy!"

I reached over and patted his shoulder. "No, you look great!" He really did. Last year he was just another skinny kid who blended into the student body. Over the summer, he had grown a few inches, and his shoulders were filling out a little.

He eyed me with suspicion.

"Really, I mean it," I said.

He sighed. "Okay, then. I guess I'm just nervous. I've spent too many years being harassed by bullies."

We pulled into a parking spot, and I turned off the engine. "That sucks. I wish I had known you back then. I would've stood up for you."

"Eh, it's okay." He waved me away. "That's nice of you, though."

We got out of the car and headed into the mass of teens surging toward the entrance.

"Jenny! Over here!"

I turned to see who was calling me, and saw Julia, Hannah, and Aya near the doors. Their long hair—light brown, blonde, and black—blew in the breeze as they fought their way back through the crowd.

"Hey!" I laughed when they all tried to hug me at once. "You're going to knock me off my feet."

"Oh my God!" Julia squealed. Can you believe this is our senior year?"

Benny stood awkwardly at my side. He fidgeted with his messenger bag.

"Hold on," Aya said, appraising Benny. "Who's the cute new guy?"

Benny's eyes widened. He looked at me, a big grin slowly spreading across his face.

"Oh, I'm sorry," I said. "This is Benny. He's not new; he's a junior this year. You probably just never had him in any of your classes."

"I'm gay," Benny blurted out. His eyebrows shot up, and he looked absolutely mortified that he had announced his sexual orientation out loud.

"Oh," Aya answered. "That's cool. Too bad though. I think hipsters are pretty hot."

I grinned at him. "See? I told you."

"Told him what?" Hannah asked.

"Nothing. Let's get to our first class. The bell's about to ring."

***

The day was almost over. Thankfully, no homework had been assigned, so my afternoon was looking pretty open.

Benny and I picked our way through the parking lot and headed toward my silvery-blue Honda Accord.

"Jenny!"

I stopped and turned toward the sound.

A blond head bobbed between the cars in the lot.

"Madeline?"

"Yeah." The petite girl finally reached us, panting. "I thought that was you. Great to see you!"

I gave her a hug. "You look awesome. Did you have a good summer?"

"Yes, I did. I was in a play over at the theatre on Mercer Island."

"I know. Your dad told me." I shifted my backpack further up on my shoulder. "Sorry I missed your show."

"Oh, that's all right. Dad told me all about your adventure in Alaska. How do you keep getting into these situations?"

I shrugged. "I don't know. But Detective Coalfield was a real asset to us. He pretty much saved our lives—until the angels showed up to help."

"I'm glad he could be there. Did you happen to see all the coverage on the news? I can't believe they didn't figure out it was you who helped find Devon."

Biting my lip, I thought about what might happen if they did find out. Luckily, my eighteenth birthday was months away—and that meant that they couldn't ask me any questions without my parents' permission until then.

She glanced at the time on her cell phone screen. "Shoot, I think I just missed the bus."

"Do you want a ride home? I'm dropping Benny off too."

"Sure. Wait, Benny?" She took a long look at him.

Benny hung back behind me, trying to melt into the pavement.

"Benny Kingston?"

"Yeah." He shrunk further into himself.

"Wow. Look at you!" Madeline stepped forward and inspected his glasses. "These are cool. Remember, we were in the same seventh grade English class together, and you barfed all over the teacher?"

"Don't remind me," he said sullenly. "That was an uncomfortable time in my life."

"And then everyone called you Barfing Benny for the rest of the year."

"Not just the next year. Someone just called me that a few months ago. I swear, people are like elephants around here—they never forget a thing."

"Well, you're not the only one," Madeline said. "I got teased because I still played with my American Girl dolls for the better part of fifth grade. They called me 'the widdle baby mama.'"

Benny grinned. "Kids can be cruel."

I unlocked the car doors. "Hop in." I started the engine and drove out of the parking lot. "What are you guys doing after school?"

"Nothing," Benny mumbled.

"I'm practicing for my audition," Madeline said from the back seat.

"Auditions aren't for another three or four weeks. Why are you rehearsing so early?" I turned left onto Coal Creek Parkway.

"It's not for a school show. It's for a couple of shows at Youth Theatre Northwest."

"The same place where you did your summer show?" I asked.

Madeline nodded. "You guys should audition too. We could be in the same production together."

I remembered how much fun I had in the last school year's production of *Into the Woods*—at least until the creepy guy stabbed Mike on opening night.

"Maybe I'll audition." I waited for the light to turn green, and then turned up the hill onto Forest Drive. "How 'bout you, Benny?"

He shook his head. "I'm not the kind of person who enjoys being the center of attention. I'm more of a behind-the-scenes kind of guy."

"You don't have to be on stage," Madeline said. "Students get to do sound or lights in the booth—or even do the backstage stuff."

Benny was quiet for a moment. "That'd be cool."

We pulled up to his small family home.

"Thanks for the ride." Benny got out. "It was nice talking to you, Madeline. Maybe I'll see you at the theatre."

She waved, got out of the backseat, and hopped into the front next to me. "That's so cool that he's your friend. I haven't had any classes with him in a super long time."

"He's kind of good at not being noticed." I drove further down the road. "I'm trying to help him come out of his shell."

"Good. Looks like you're doing a fine job so far."

I pulled up to her house and stopped the car.

She got out and leaned in through the open door. "Need any help with your audition material?"

"Nope. I think I've got it down now. But thanks for offering."

Chapter 3

My stomach twisted, and my mouth went dry. I had no idea what to expect with this audition. I assumed it would be somewhat similar to the ones at school, and I was a nervous wreck for those.

The colorful show posters painted on the cinder block walls caught my attention. Standing before the painted images of *42nd Street, Romeo and Juliet*, and Disney's *Aladdin Jr.*, I wished I had prepared just a little more. I wiped my palms on my jeans and scanned the form in my hand to make sure I had filled in all the information.

I opened the doors to the lobby and took a deep breath. There were dozens of students lined up at the table, signing in, and getting their audition numbers. Several others were huddled in small groups talking excitedly about which shows they were auditioning for and what shows they had done together in the past.

The line moved fairly quickly. Madeline had already done her audition the day before, so I was left alone, without a familiar face to keep me company. I reached the front of the line and handed in my paperwork and headshot.

"Thanks," the guy behind the desk said, taking the paperwork from me. "I'm Miguel." He stretched his hand out for a handshake. "Go ahead and make yourself comfortable. We'll call you when you're up."

My feet padded across the rich burgundy and gold carpet. I sat down on the wooden bench in the middle of the lobby and glanced around. There were old photos of students in various productions throughout the years hanging high up on the walls. The vibes in this building were good. I said a silent prayer that I would be cast in a show here.

I took my phone out of my bag and pretended to scroll through my Instagram feed while I waited.

"Jenny Crumb." Miguel stood up and motioned toward the door. His pinstriped vest looked freshly pressed. "They're ready for you."

"Thanks," I muttered, trying to steady my nerves.

He opened the big double doors to the theatre and led me inside. Nine or ten adults sat in a row of seats midway up; a long table stretched out in front of them. They turned to look at me.

"Give your sheet music to Emma," Miguel whispered.

The woman at the piano turned to give me a smile and waved me over. I showed her the sixteen bars that I would be singing, and she marked it on the score with a pencil. "Are you ready?"

"I think so." I walked onto the stage and stared out into the audience. My palms started to sweat. I could feel my heart picking up the pace inside my chest. They waited expectantly.

"Go ahead," one of the directors said.

I cleared my throat. "Hi, my name is Jenny Crumb, and I'm seventeen years old. I'll be singing 'Not for the Life of Me' from *Thoroughly Modern Millie*, and I'll be doing a monologue from *The Secret Garden*."

Once I started singing, my nerves settled down. I somehow finished the song and the monologue without forgetting the words to either.

"Thank you." My muscles tensed, and I stood like a deer caught in headlights.

"Thank you, Jenny."

"Oh, right." I exited down the stage stairs and glanced back.

The directors had their heads buried in their notes.

Blowing out a breath of relief, I went to collect my sheet music from the pianist. "Great job," Emma whispered.

"Thanks." My stomach unclenched and I felt a little better.

I walked out into the lobby where Miguel was waiting. "How did it go?"

"Fine, I think." The butterflies in my stomach hadn't yet stopped fluttering.

"Callbacks will be posted on our website on Friday."

Friday. I only had to wait two days until I got the news.

He stapled some paperwork together. "Your name won't appear on the list, just your callback number. If you have an X under the shows that you auditioned for, that means you're called back. If there're no Xs, that means you aren't called back." He saw the look on my face. "Oh, don't worry. I'm sure you did great. And even if you aren't called back, we offer some really good classes to help you get ready for the next auditions."

I swallowed. "Okay, thank you."

Outside, I took a moment to regroup. Did I do all right? Auditioning for the school play was one thing. But auditioning for a real theatre organization was quite another.

The breeze kicked up again. A wisp of breath tickled my neck. What was that? I whirled around. No one was there. Maybe I had just imagined it.

***

Sitting at the desk in my room, I hit the refresh button on my laptop again. It was after school on Friday, and callbacks were supposed to be uploaded to the website already.

12

Refresh.

Nothing.

Refresh.

Nothing.

Refresh. Something was loading! The screen filled in from top to bottom. I bit my lip and glanced at my form. My audition number was ninety-six.

The first set of numbers loaded.

Refresh.

My eyes scanned down the numbers until I reached mine. There! I was called back for *42nd Street* and *Romeo and Juliet*. Jumping up from my chair, I squealed and did a happy dance.

Feet pounded up the stairs. "Jenny, are you all right?" My mom appeared in the doorway.

"I'm more than all right!" I shouted. "I got called back."

"At the theatre?"

"Yup."

Mom watched, her mouth hanging open, as I did another happy dance. My feet skittered across the carpet in a grapevine formation. Hopping into the air, I hollered and slid into the splits.

"Let me guess." Mom chuckled. "You're pretty excited about this."

I fell back onto the floor, my arms spread wide, and grinned up at the ceiling. "Yes, you could say that."

She stepped into my room and extended her hand. "Since you're in such a great mood, I bet you won't mind helping me get dinner started."

Buzz kill. I reached my hand out to her, and she hoisted me off the floor.

"I guess. What are we having?" I pulled on my hoodie.

"Soup and salad." Mom followed me down the stairs.

We got to work in the kitchen. I was lighter than air, still feeling the effects of the good news. My feet floated across the tiled floor as I moved between the sink and the chopping board.

The door to the garage opened and Dad and Jackson appeared. Dad hugged me and headed into the family room. Jackson surveyed the commotion in the kitchen.

"What's for dinner?" my brother asked. He was in sixth grade this year; the most obnoxious year for boys in middle school.

"Chicken noodle soup and a salad." Mom hugged him and wiped a smudge of dirt off his face. "How do you get so dirty all the time?"

Jackson shrugged. "Soccer."

Because I was in a better than normal mood, I glanced at Jackson without making an unkind remark. I noted that he had grown several inches in just a short while. He seemed to take up more space in the room. His sandy hair was tousled, but not in the usual, mangy way. My little brother was not so little anymore. He was growing up.

"What are you lookin' at?" He narrowed his eyes, glaring at me suspiciously.

"Nothing. Just noticing that you don't look as ridiculous as usual." I grabbed a cucumber off the counter and began peeling it.

A look of confusion crossed his face. "Thanks?"

Mom made a faux gasping noise. "Wait. Are you actually—kind of—getting along?"

Jackson rolled his eyes. "Don't think that's possible."

"He's right. Not possible." I hid my smile as I sliced the cucumber.

Mom sighed. "Ah, well. One can dream."

14

Chapter 4

"Wheeee!" Our voices went up high, following the voice of the musical director, Jan. "Ohhhhhhh." The sound dipped down the scale. "Nnnnnnnn, mmnnnnn, yummmm."

I felt silly doing these exercises. But everyone else was doing them, and it was part of the callback.

"Yummmmm," we echoed. "Yum, yum, yum, yum, yum."

"Good." Jan slid her glasses back up her nose. She sat back down at the piano. "Listen to this song first, then I'll have you sing. It's called 'Lullaby of Broadway', and the music is by Al Dubin and Harry Warren." She plunked out the first few bars of introduction, and then sang the beginning verses. Her rich voice echoed after the last note. "Ready to try?" she asked.

Jan led us through the song, haltingly at first. Then, as we caught on, she picked up the tempo. She lined us up across the stage. We each took a turn singing as she pointed to us one at a time. My nerves weren't as jacked-up as they had been during the initial audition, and my voice came out strong and clear. She smiled at me and nodded, and then pointed to the subsequent person.

Next, she explained the context of the show. She had us make facial expressions and body and hand motions as we sang. "Now sing it happier," she yelled. We smiled and sang with saccharine glee.

15

Satisfied, she sat back down at the director's table.

Another woman got up. "Some of you know me already, but for those who don't, my name is Lea, and I'm the choreographer. I just wanted to clarify something before we jump into dancing. When you do a musical, there are three key people you'll be working with: your director, Meg." She pointed to a woman wearing a gray cardigan. "Of course, your musical director, Jan, and your choreographer; that's me. Clear?"

We nodded.

Her chin-length curly hair bounced when she walked. "*42nd Street* is all about tap dancing. How many of you have tap danced before?"

Only a few students raised their hands. For once, I was glad Mom had made me take tap lessons when I was younger. I still remembered some of the steps.

Lea acknowledged those of us who had put our hands up. "You'll have a slight advantage for sure, but for the rest of you, don't worry about it. This is a conservatory. That means that you'll have a class once a week for several months before rehearsals even begin. During class time, we'll be working mostly on tap, so you'll all be able to do the steps."

The girl next to me relaxed her shoulders. "Good," she whispered.

Lea showed us a simple combination of tap steps to go with the music. It seemed like we tapped forever until she was satisfied.

"Now, let's see you in small groups. You five go first." She pointed to a group of kids on the end.

The music started up, and the actors did their best to tap out the rhythm. A tall boy in the group struggled. Most of the students didn't have tap shoes, so it was more difficult for them. When it was my turn, I breezed through the combination. My confidence had crept back up, and my nervousness dissipated.

"That was great!" Lea said when everyone had a turn. "I'm so impressed with all of you. You're putting in so much effort—that's what I like to see. I don't care if you're the best tap dancer in the world; if your heart isn't in it, the audience can feel it. But if you're giving it your all, the audience will believe you. They'll believe your characters. *That's* what's important."

A cold breeze flitted past my shoulder, snapping me out of my reverie. I shivered.

"Wonderful job, everyone." Meg, the director stood up from her seat and approached the stage. She turned back to the musical director and choreographer. "And thank *you*, ladies. Great job with the music and dance." She walked up the short staircase to the stage. "Let's do some scene work."

***

The next day, callbacks for *Romeo and Juliet* began at six o'clock. I got there just as the stage manager opened the doors to the theatre. The students waiting in the lobby stampeded past me.

"You had better sign in." It was the same guy who had signed us in for the auditions.

"Hi, Miguel." I mentally patted myself on the back for remembering his name.

"Hey, there." He smiled at me and handed me the clipboard.

I scrawled my name on the sheet. "Thanks." I thrust the clipboard at him and rushed through the doors.

I looked at the students filling up the seats and spotted Madeline. There was an empty one next to her.

"Hey." I slid into the chair.

"Jenny, I'm so glad you're here." She hugged me. "I haven't seen you at school since the first day."

"I know. Wish we had some classes together." I shoved my bag under my seat.

"Shakespeare should be a challenge," she said. "Have you ever done any of his plays?"

"Nope. But I took Classic Literature last year, and we read a lot of his work."

"Lucky." She pulled her hoodie off and stuffed it into her backpack. "I haven't done any Shakespeare yet. I'm worried that I'll fall on my face."

"You'll be fine," I assured her.

Miguel asked us to run through a theatre game to get us warmed up. "How many of you have played 'What are you doing?"

The majority of the actors raised their hands. My hand was not.

"There are a few of you who haven't. Let me explain the rules." Miguel walked to center stage. "Let's have all of you up here and form a circle."

Once we were all in our places, he pointed to a boy. "Ross, you've played this lots of times. You'll start." He spoke to the rest of us. "The first person will start doing an action." He pointed to Ross, who began miming mowing the lawn.

Miguel pointed to the person next to Ross. "The person to your right will ask, 'what are you doing?'"

The girl next to Ross said, "What are you doing?"

"Then the person doing the action says something that is completely different than his actions." Miguel pointed to Ross.

"I'm brushing my teeth," Ross said.

"Then," Miguel continued, "The person who asked him the question begins to do the action the first person said."

The girl mimed brushing her teeth. Miguel pointed to the person to her right.

"What are you doing?" the big guy next to her said.

"I'm taking a nap," the girl answered.

"And so on and so on," Miguel said. "Ready to play?

By the time we finished the game, we were all laughing and feeling more at ease.

"Everyone can take a seat," Miguel said.

A distinguished-looking man sauntered up the steps to the stage. The auditorium quieted down; all eyes were on him. He was tall and sported glasses and a goatee. "Welcome, I'm Jack, your director," he said. "This is a good turn-out for callbacks. I'm pleased."

Miguel walked onto the stage with a packet of scripts.

The director continued. "I know many of you have never read Shakespeare, so I don't want you to worry if you stumble over the words. I promise you it will sound like a foreign language at first, but once you start reading, you'll eventually understand what you're saying."

We glanced at each other nervously.

"I'd like to start with the first scene. Let's see you, you, you, and you." He pointed to various students.

The scene opened with members of the Capulet and Montague families nearly getting into a brawl. I had recently seen *West Side Story* at the Paramount Theatre, and this reminded me of the showdown between the rival gangs. I marveled at how some of the actors were able to let the language roll off their tongues, while others couldn't even get out a sentence without tripping over the words.

"Why don't we move onto a scene with *Romeo and Juliet*?" He pointed to a boy that was sitting on the other side of the auditorium. "Let's have you as Romeo." Jack peered over the rest of the students in the audience. "And you as Juliet." He pointed to me.

Oh. My. God. I wasn't prepared for this.

"What's your name?" he asked me.

"Jenny."

"Jenny, meet Caleb—your Romeo."

"Nice to meet you, Caleb." I smiled apprehensively at him.

"Likewise."

"This is the kissing scene from the great hall at the Capulets," Jack explained.

The students snickered.

Oh, crap.

"I apologize for putting you two through this. And I want you to know that I almost *never* work on kissing scenes for callbacks. Usually, this happens during the rehearsal process while we are working on the actual scenes and everyone has had a chance to get to know one another." The director ran his fingers through his hair.

Horror. This was sheer horror. I bit my lip and watched Caleb's eyebrows scrunch up.

"But there has to be chemistry between Romeo and Juliet. Otherwise, the audience won't believe it. I have to be sure that the kids I cast as the tragic lovers have a spark. The audience has to believe they are in love." Jack observed our body language and chuckled. "I sure made you uncomfortable, didn't I?"

Caleb looked as nervous as I felt. Although he was several inches taller than me, he seemed to shrink down to my height. I kind of liked him for it. And as I studied him more carefully, I realized that he looked a little like my friend, Cassandra. His short wavy hair was the same auburn color as hers.

"Tell you what," Jack said. "How 'bout if we just do the scene as naturally as possible. And when it comes time for the kiss, you will have the option of actually kissing each other, or maybe just a hug will do. Either way, make it believable."

I looked down at my feet. This sucked, but actors had to do this sort of thing all the time, right? Would Caleb kiss me or would he hug me instead? I should've had a mint before I got up on stage. My heart was pounding. What was Caleb feeling?

Celine had recently given me a lesson in tuning into people's energy. I felt guilty trying—it seemed like an invasion of privacy. Celine had warned me about using this ability. It wasn't something that should be used too often, and only in dire situations. She always talked about the responsibility of having this gift, and wanted me to maintain the highest integrity. But I'd never tried it out before, and I desperately wanted to know what he was thinking.

I banished my guilt, took a deep breath, and zeroed in on the emotions emanating from his body. And did just as Celine had taught me… I tuned into his energy.

Oh my God, oh my God, oh my God.

I've never kissed a girl before.

Why didn't I have a mint before I came up here?

Will she kiss me or will she hug me?

I hid my smile. At least he wasn't a smug bastard. He was feeling the same things I was. Okay, I was going to do this and give it my best shot. What was the worst thing that could happen? We could bump noses. It could be awful and embarrassing. Everyone might laugh at us. They would tease us. I thought maybe I could handle most of those things. If we pulled off the scene, we would each have a stellar part. Who wouldn't want to be Romeo or Juliet?

"Let's begin." Jack arranged us on stage. "The scene takes place at the home of the Capulets. It's a masquerade ball. Romeo is attending in disguise, and it's the only way that he would ever be able to set foot in the Capulet home. You see, the Capulets and the Montagues are feuding."

Caleb shifted his feet.

Jack handed us our scripts marked with colored post-it notes. "Here you go. Start from this line here." He pointed to the top of the page.

We quickly reviewed the text.

Caleb cleared his throat. *"My lips, two blushing pilgrims, ready stand, to smooth that rough touch with a tender kiss."*

It was my turn. *"Good pilgrim, you do wrong your hand too much, which mannerly devotion shows in this; for*

21

saints have hands that pilgrims' hands do touch, And palm to palm is holy palmers' kiss."

I shivered. The air conditioning must have kicked on.

"Have not saints lips, and holy palmers too?" Caleb stepped forward and took my hand.

He was good.

"Ay, pilgrim, lips that they must use in prayer." I laced my fingers through his. I gave him a shy look.

"O, then, dear saint, let lips do what hands do; they pray, grant thou, lest faith turn to despair." He kissed my hand.

I curtsied to him and batted my eyelashes. The other actors whooped from the audience. *"Saints do not move, though grant for prayers' sake."*

"Then move not, while my prayer's effect I take. Thus from my lips, by yours, my sin is purged." He stepped closer to me. I felt the tremble in his hand, but his expression remained in character. I realized how good this kid was. He had never kissed a girl before, but he was playing this part like a pro.

He pulled me in and tilted my chin up. I could see near panic in his dark brown eyes. He seemed to fight his fear, and then kissed me gently on the lips.

I ignored the cold breeze wrapping itself around my shoulders, and stepped back from him and grinned.

"Bravo!" Jack said, clapping his hands.

The actors erupted into more whoops and cat calls.

"Well done." The director looked at us approvingly. Then he looked out into the audience. "We need another pair to audition for Romeo and Juliet. Would anyone else like to give that a try?"

Chapter 5

It was dark when I came out of the theatre. I waved to Detective Coalfield, who was waiting for Madeline in the parking lot. After I slipped into my seat and closed my car door, the screen on my phone lit up and it buzzed. It was a text from Cassandra, my Alaskan friend from Sitka Fine Arts Camp.

"I'm coming to Seattle!"

"Really?" I couldn't believe it. I wasn't sure I'd get to see her again. "Why? When?" I tapped on my screen.

"Need new clothes for the school year. Coming down to shop and visit UW. I'm applying for next year."

"Awesome!" I typed, thinking about how much fun it would be to see her again.

"Guess what else?"

"I give up. What else?"

"Ty is coming with me!"

I sat in stunned silence. Ty? Why would he take a trip with Cassandra?

"He's coming down for the same reasons. New clothes and applying to UW."

A strange feeling came over me. This was like when two worlds collided. My summer in Sitka felt like it took place in another world, in another time. My life here was so separate from that. Now that they would be bumping together, I didn't know how to feel about it.

"Back together with Mike?" Cassandra texted.

Good question. "Not sure."

"Huh?"

"I think he wants to get back together…"

"But you're still mad at him?"

"Kind of. And school just started. No time to hang out with him."

Oh my God. Ty and Cassandra would be visiting the UW campus. What if they ran into Mike?

"It would be cool to meet him!" she texted.

"I don't think so."

"Because of Ty?"

"Yeah." I shuddered. The thought of Ty running into Mike did not please me.

"But Ty didn't want a relationship. It will be fine," she wrote.

"Still… awkward."

"Gotta go! Dinner's ready. Text you later with details."

"Bye." I set my phone back down on my seat.

The phone lit up again, like there was another text coming through, but it was blank. Huh. That was strange. The screen went dark again.

I started up the engine. Hopefully, the heater would start kicking in some warm air soon.

***

After dinner, I helped Mom with the dishes.

"Have any homework tonight?" She put the last plate in the dishwasher.

"Just some reading for my Language and Composition class." I poured myself a cup of hot water from the tea kettle.

"Dad and I are going to take Jackson to the Sounders game tomorrow night. Are you okay here by yourself?"

"Mom, I'm almost eighteen. Of course I'll be all right!" I put a tea bag in my cup and let it sink to the bottom.

24

"I know, I know," Mom said with a guilty grin. "I can't help being a little protective of you after all that's happened in the last year."

"I'll be fine. There are no crazy kidnappers coming after me at the moment. I don't think you have to worry about anything."

"Good. Then I won't worry." She hugged me. "I'm going up to my office. Don't stay up too late, okay?"

"Okay." I squirted some honey into my tea and stirred it. My phone buzzed in my pocket.

It was Mike "Have time to talk?"

I hesitated. "I guess."

"Call you."

My phone rang. "Hi."

"Hi. Sorry I haven't had a chance to talk to you. I've been moving my stuff into my dorm already."

"When do classes start?" I wondered how long we'd have to do this small talk thing before he brought up getting back together. I still wasn't sure what I wanted.

"Next week. But I'm here for freshman orientation, and I'm auditioning for the first show of the year."

"Oh." I didn't know what else to say.

"Are you free this weekend?"

I bit my lip. Mike had a magnetic hold on my heart. But when he told me that he didn't want a girlfriend his freshman year in college, it had hurt me. I knew it was because his dad had convinced him of that, but it had still wounded me. I was in love with him. Rejection was a tough pill to swallow, especially because I was so invested in the relationship. Still, what if we could pick up where we left off?

"I'm free." I twisted a strand of my hair.

"Great! How 'bout if I pick you up on Saturday night. Say around six o'clock?"

"Sure."

"I can't wait to see you." The sound of his voice made my heart skip a beat.

I hesitated. "Same here."

Chapter 6

"Are you sure it's not up yet?" She bit her thumbnail anxiously.

It was Friday. Madeline and I were huddled around my laptop. We had successfully broken the world record for hitting the refresh button one hundred and fifty times in a thirty minute period.

I hit F5 on my keyboard one more time. "Hey!" I shouted.

The list began populating the screen until the entire page loaded. "Which one should I check first?" I turned to look at my friend. Her unblinking eyes were glued to the monitor.

"Check *Romeo and Juliet*. We both auditioned for that one."

Our eyes searched the number field and the corresponding Xs in the columns with the roles.

"Oh my God!" I squealed. "I got Juliet."

Madeline whooped and hugged me.

I turned back to the monitor. "Let's see what you got."

"There." She pointed at number eighty-nine. "Capulet's wife."

"Woohoo!" I yelled. "Wait, you're playing my mother?"

"Ha—it's probably not a big part, but as your mom, I get to tell you what to do." A grin lit up her face.

27

"Okay, what else did you audition for?" I asked.

"Just *Aladdin*. *42ⁿᵈ Street* didn't work with my schedule."

"Let's see if you got into *Aladdin* then." I clicked on the link.

"Hmmm, I got the narrator role." She shrugged. "That's okay, I guess."

"I'm sure it will be fun. Anything else?"

"Nope. I wanted to keep my schedule open for the school play in the spring. How 'bout you?"

I clicked on the *42ⁿᵈ Street* link and searched for my audition number. "I got Dorothy. That's a pretty good role. I knew I wouldn't get Peggy—it requires a much better tap dancer than me."

"Well, I think we did pretty well." Madeline got up from my bed. "Let's celebrate. Frozen yogurt?"

"I'll get my car keys," I said.

***

On Saturday morning, I slept in until past noon.

When I got downstairs, the kitchen was deserted. Evidence of breakfast lay strewn throughout the room. The sink was filled with pans, bowls, and whisks. Yellow batter of some sort spotted the dark granite kitchen counters. Then I remembered that Jackson had an early soccer game. My parents must have both gone to watch him play.

I sighed and opened the refrigerator to see if there was anything edible in it. A plate of French toast was on the second shelf, wrapped in plastic, and had a note attached.

"Jenny—went to Jackson's soccer game. See you this afternoon. Love you! Mom."

At least I could always count on my mom to feed me. Microwaved French toast was gross, so I opted to put it in the oven. I set the plate on the counter, and waited for the oven to heat up. I poured myself a cup of coffee and rubbed the sleep out of my eyes.

Saturday was my favorite day of the week. No school, and the promise of an entire weekend of—wait! Saturday. I was going on a date with Mike.

I shuffled to the downstairs powder room as quickly as my slippers would allow. I peered into the mirror. My hair was a mess of tangles. Bed-head did not become me. Was that a zit forming on my chin? Gah! This was not happening. Hopefully, I had some emergency pimple cream in my make-up bag.

The oven beeped. I had time to eat. Mike was picking me up at six o'clock, but there was so much to do before then.

I high-speed shuffled back to the kitchen and threw the plate of toast in. Even a date with Mike wouldn't stop me from eating breakfast. I set the timer for ten minutes. My mind raced, mentally picking through all the clothes in my closet.

The blue sweater? No, too last year. And I was wearing blue when he broke up with me during the summer. Maybe my little black dress. Too formal. What if he took me to a football game or something? Ugh. I had no clothes at all. That was it—I was having a fashion crisis.

I took off my slippers and ran up the stairs, dodged through the hallway, and into my room. I grabbed my cell phone and flew down the stairs. There was only one person who could help me. The buzzer on the oven dinged. I grabbed an oven mitt and pulled the plate out, rummaged through the fridge again and snagged the bottle of maple syrup.

Only a girlfriend could help me. I held my phone up to my ear and wolfed a bite of French toast down as it rang on the other end.

"Hello?" Benny said.

"Benny, I need you!"

"Um, this is awkward. You do know that I'm gay, right? Although, I'm flattered and all, but …"

"Benny! This is an emergency."

"Wow, sounds like you are really hot and bothered. Can't you call Mike or somebody else to help you out?"

I rolled my eyes. "Will you stop? I have a date with Mike tonight, I have no clothes to wear, and I have a zit on my chin the size of Texas."

Benny snorted. "And I'm supposed to, what, help you pop it or something?"

"Ew! Gross. No, I need you to go shopping with me. Then I have to get to the make-up counter at Nordstrom's to see if they have some heavy-duty concealer."

"I'm still not sure why you want *me* to come with you."

"Because I need an outfit that is not too casual, not too formal, and sexy, but not too sexy, because I'm not sure if I really want to get back together with Mike, but I want him to think I'm kinda hot, but not too hot, if you know what I mean, and you're a guy and so you'll give me the guy's perspective so I can—"

"You had better slow down. It's like you have diarrhea of the mouth."

I blew out a breath.

"Okay. I'll be right over."

I smiled and ended the call. My stomach rumbled. I checked my watch. Just two minutes to wolf down the rest of my breakfast.

***

Benny showed up a few minutes after I had finished getting dressed.

"Glad you're not wearing that tonight," he remarked after he took a look at my faded jeans and the Newport Knights t-shirt.

I shrugged. "That's why I need your help." I locked the door behind us. "Which store should we go to first? Hollister or Abercrombie?"

"Aren't they the same thing?"

"You have a point. Let's go with American Eagle."

***

"Mom, can you help me set up a visit to the U-Dub?" I asked. "Cassandra and Ty are coming down from Sitka to visit the university soon. I'd like to go with them when they're here."

"Okay. Do you know the exact day?"

"Not yet. But I'll text Cassandra to get the details."

"I thought you didn't want to apply to the University of Washington, though," she said. "We visited so many schools on the East Coast last year. I thought you were set on moving far, far away from here."

I laughed. "It just seemed so appealing to go somewhere, you know, exotic."

"You call the East Coast exotic?"

"Anywhere but Seattle is exotic to me."

Mom patted me on the shoulder. "Trust me, I get it. I wanted to go to Northwestern in Chicago for college."

"Why didn't you?"

"My dad talked me out of it. He didn't want me to leave the state."

"Yeah, you've always said you were a daddy's girl." I smiled.

"Where is Mike taking you on your date?" Mom asked.

"I don't know yet." I took my cell phone off its charger and slipped it into my pocket.

"Well, you sure look cute," Mom said. "Hope you didn't spend too much."

I looked down at my pink top and dark skinny jeans. "The top was a clearance item. They're stocking the stores with fall and winter clothing."

"Good job. Are those new earrings?"

I rolled my eyes. "Mother ..." The noise of an engine made me peek out the window. "He's here. Bye, Mom." I rushed out the door and waved at her before it closed.

Mike's shiny black car idled at the curb. He got out of the vehicle and approached me.

"You look great." His smile lit up his face, and his green eyes danced in the sunlight. God, he was so sexy. I swallowed. I still wasn't sure if I wanted to get back together. Better to wait and see how the evening played out.

He held out his arms for a hug. I tentatively stepped in and gave him a quick, friendly hug. The disappointment registered on his face when I pulled away. He opened the door for me, and I slipped inside the air-conditioned car.

"It's so good to see you, Jenny." The car rolled to a stop at the light. He gave me an awkward smile, and reached over to squeeze my hand.

I turned to look at him. There was just a hint of stubble on his jawline. "Good to see you too. So—where are you taking me?"

The light turned green. He was silent a moment as we pulled onto Coal Creek Parkway. His lips curved into the smile that used to drive me crazy—and apparently, still did. "Is it okay if I keep you out kind of late?"

"I guess so. But where are we going?"

"Dinner at Salty's on Alki, and then a walk on the beach at sunset."

I gasped. He was pulling out all the stops. That was way beyond the scope of most of our dates. I tried looking nonchalant. "That sounds—nice."

"Is it too much?" He furrowed his brow. "Would you rather go get fish and chips at Spud's?"

I remembered how noisy it was the last time I had been to Spud's—lots of families with young kids. "No, it's not too much. I'd like that, actually."

"Salty's it is, then."

***

The hostess led us to a two-person table on the deck. The September evening was still holding onto its summer warmth. The view was incredible. Downtown Seattle shone in the early evening sun. The blue of the Puget Sound water put me at ease.

"The waitress will be right over to get your drink orders."

"Thank you," both Mike and I answered.

We ordered iced teas, and she handed us our dinner menus.

Mike ignored the menu and reached across the table for my hand. I instinctively pulled it away, and then realized my rudeness.

"I'm sorry," I said when I saw how crushed he looked.

"No, no, it's all right." He lowered his eyes to the menu. "I shouldn't assume anything."

I bit my lip. "It's just that I don't know how I feel about us. Not yet, at least."

"I understand. Listen, Jenny, I really screwed up this summer. I let my dad dictate what I should do with my life. It was stupid and immature of me to listen to him. I have regretted it every second of every day since you left for Alaska." He looked so desperate, I immediately felt sorry for him.

"I know that your dad didn't want you to have a relationship your freshman year of college. I just don't want to create a rift between you and him. You might end up resenting me for it someday." I had such conflicting emotions running through me. I wanted to be angry with

33

Mike for caving in to his dad's wishes, but I also understood that he needed to please his parents. My parents' approval was important to me too. But then again, Mike was eighteen. He should stand up for himself and what he wanted.

"I could never resent you, Jenny. All I can say is that I'm sorry." He looked into my eyes. "I promise, if you give me another chance, I will make it up to you."

"Part of the reason I was so attracted to you," I said, "was that you seemed so strong and sure of yourself. But then you gave into your dad so easily. It made me worry that you're not the guy I thought you were." It was so uncomfortable to confront him like this, but I had to be honest.

Mike looked down at the table and shook his head slightly. "I know. I was wrong." He looked back up. "But can we see where this goes?"

He wasn't giving up on me. That showed he had some sort of strength at least. I let myself smile. "Okay, but let's slow this way down. Can we just start over?"

"Start over? What do you mean?"

"I mean, we can pretend that this is our first date and that we are not 'together,' not yet." I bit my lip. I was not going to jump in with both feet like I did last time. Protecting my heart was important. I wouldn't allow someone to break it so easily again.

Mike's expression was hopeful. "So, you'll give me another chance?"

"I suppose so; but please, like I said before, this is our first date. There are no guarantees."

The breath he let out scared a seagull off the railing of the deck, and his grin lit up his face. He reached out his right hand. "Hi, Jenny. I'm Mike. Nice to meet you."

I took his hand in mine and shook it. "Nice to meet you too."

My cell phone buzzed in my pocket. I took it out and frowned. "Huh."

"What?" Mike asked.

"Oh, it's nothing," I answered. "My phone has been acting up lately. It's probably time for a new one."

***

The walk on the beach was romantic. I took off my shoes and carried them in one hand. The last rays of the evening sun warmed the sand beneath my feet.

"So, I never got a chance to ask you," Mike said as he walked alongside me. "How was Alaska?"

"Oh, it was great. I mean, lots of stuff happened." I thought of the search for Devon, and finding him alive. Thoughts of River came next, and how I had found her dead inside the little makeshift shelter on Whale Island. More thoughts jumbled through my mind; Cassandra, Ty, his raven tattoo, the connection we shared.

"Like what?"

I debated on whether or not I should spill the entire story. A ferry horn sounded in the distance.

Mike studied my face. "You look like you're fighting a battle in your head; like a million things are going on behind those blue eyes of yours."

I sighed. "Maybe you're a little bit psychic too." I led him to a log, washed white from the sun, and sat down. I patted the spot next to me. "Sit."

Then, I told him everything.

Chapter 7

Romeo and Juliet rehearsals started up on Monday. I had driven home from school and had eaten a quick dinner.

Madeline and I filed into the lobby with everyone else who was cast.

"Hey, Jenny." Caleb, the kid who I had to kiss at callbacks nudged me with his elbow.

"Oh, hi." I smiled at him. "What part did you get? Romeo?"

"Yeah." His cheeks dimpled. "And you?"

"Juliet."

"Ah, I guess our kiss was convincing enough then." His face reddened.

Well, this was awkward. If I agreed, he'd probably think I liked him.

"Sign in, you guys." Miguel handed us the clipboard.

The cast was fairly small so it didn't take long for everyone to check in.

Jack, the director, stood in the pit and leaned up against the stage. His face brightened when he saw Caleb and me. "Congratulations, you two!"

I stole a glance at Caleb. The blush bloomed again on his cheeks.

Jack climbed up on the stage and motioned for all of us to take our seats. He was remarkably spry for a man his age.

He was older than my dad, but in better shape. My dad had a little tiny pot belly and bad knees.

"First of all, I'd like to congratulate you for getting cast in the show," Jack said. "As with all other shows, I'll have Miguel lead you through some warm-ups. Then we'll do a read-through of the play."

Miguel called us up to the stage area. "We are going to do a warm-up called 'Emotion Party.' Does everyone know how to play that?"

Several students laughed and nudged each other. I had never played this one before, so I felt kind of clueless.

"Basically, we start with the host of the party—who has a neutral emotion. The guest will ring the doorbell, then walk in with a charged emotion. So, emotions that work well are ones like, jealousy, hatred, joy, fear, sadness, excitement... you get the picture?"

I nodded along with everyone else.

"Good. Then the host 'catches' the emotion and interacts with the guest in the same manner. Each guest enters with a different emotion and that new emotion slowly spreads throughout the party guests."

"This ought to be good," I whispered to Madeline.

"Sydney," Miguel said. "You can be the host."

She stood on stage while everyone else stood in the wings.

Madeline was the first guest. "Ding dong!"

Sydney pretended to open the door.

"Hi, oh my God!" Madeline jumped up and down, grinning from ear to ear.

Sydney started jumping and smiling too. "Oh my God!" she shrieked.

"This is so awesome! I love parties!"

"Me too!" They grabbed hands and jumped up and down.

"Ding dong!" The next guest had arrived.

"Hello," a girl wearing a black hoodie and yoga pants said. She cast her eyes downward and pretended to wipe a tear away.

"Hello." She was led into the party. When Madeline saw the girl, her grin disappeared.

The girl's shoulders sagged, and she sniffled. Madeline and Sydney sat down on the stage looking deflated and dejected.

"Ding dong." It was Caleb. "Ugh! I can't believe I'm late to the party. This is awful! There was an accident on the way and I had to sit in traffic for an hour!" he roared. "Why does this always happen to me?" He stomped his feet.

Just as everyone was adjusting to the new emotion, another door bell sounded.

When Sydney opened the door, a tall girl entered. "Who are you?" The girl looked at her suspiciously. "Why are you in my boyfriend's house? He said he wanted to go home early to take a nap. I didn't think a floozy like you would be here!" She stormed in. "I said, who *are* you?"

"I'm his girlfriend, who are *you*?" Madeline eyed the girl up and down.

The tall girl shoved Madeline and jealousy spread to the rest of the party-goers.

The actors still in the wings started laughing.

"Ding dong!"

Sydney opened the door. A short boy with tousled hair said, "Woohoo! We won! This is the best day of my life!" He grabbed the tall girl, but she was still in her jealous rage… and so was everyone else. I looked around to each guest at the party and they were still shoving each other and accusing one another of cheating.

"What the heck?" I looked at Miguel, who had a confused look on his face.

"Hey, guys, tone it down." He stepped into the circle, but was shoved from behind by Caleb.

This wasn't making any sense. Even the guy who had come in last was joining the jealousy parade.

"Whoa!" The director yelled from the audience. "That's enough!"

This seemed to snap people out of whatever it was they were doing. Some of them still looked angry, but a few were looking sheepish; like they knew they were doing something odd, but couldn't quite place what it was.

"Now, I know you guys are really good actors, but you have to know when to stop and not take it too far," Jack said, crossing his arms.

"Sorry," mumbled Caleb. "I don't know how that happened."

Jack chuckled. "Well, try to have just a little more control over your emotions next time. Tell you what—let's do a read-through. Everyone, grab your scripts."

While people were getting scripts and bottles of water from their packs, I glanced at their faces, trying to figure out the sudden surge of bad emotions. What had gotten into them?

I pulled off my hoodie and stuffed it in my bag. My phone caught my eye. I quickly grabbed it to turn off the ringer. An Instagram alert appeared on my lock screen. I opened the app to see what it was. There was a notification in my direct message box. What the heck? Nobody ever used direct messages on Instagram. I touched the little icon to open it. Some random dude had sent me a black square instead of a photo. The message with the square said, "Hi, beautiful." Who was this? I didn't recognize the weird name, cbrj84. I shrugged. Somebody must've followed me on Instagram by mistake. I really needed to check my privacy settings.

***

After rehearsal, I lay in my bed, texting Cassandra.

"When are you and Ty coming?"

"Tuesday, Nov. 4th," she texted back.

"That's the week of our show opening. Can you come see it?"

"What show?"

"*Romeo and Juliet*. RJ for short."

"Cool. We'll come."

"Yay!"

I glanced at the pile of homework on my desk. A pang of guilt hit me.

"Gotta go. Homework."

"Bye."

I got up and turned on my laptop. I opened my Word document and started editing my English paper.

***

It was late. My essay was done, my math homework in the bag, and I was beat. I got ready for bed and snuggled down under the covers. Overall, it had been a good day. I yawned and closed my eyes.

"Romeo?" I gazed at him lying on the black wood of the stage, an empty cup lying on its side next to him. "Romeo."

I kissed him gently. "Thy lips are warm." But no breath spurred the rise and fall of his chest. This was not right. There, his dagger in its sheath. I wrenched it from his side. Wait. No. This was not right. I could not do it.

Romeo, his lips now a cruel shade of blue, sat up. His glassy eyes narrowed upon me. "Join me, Juliet. You promised."

I bolted upright in bed. The sheets were tangled around my legs. My breath hitched in my chest, and tears rolled down my cheeks. Thank God. It was only a dream.

I was groggy when I arrived at school the next morning. My restless night was not helping me.

Benny stood by his locker, working his combination with a frown.

"What's up? Forget your combo?"

"No," he said indignantly. He worked the dial again. "Okay, maybe I did." He yawned and rubbed his eyes.

"You too?" I stifled a yawn.

Benny gave me the once-over. "Guess I'm not the only one who lost some sleep last night. You look like hell."

"Thanks. So do you."

"What kept you up?" He finally got the combination right and the lock sprang open.

"Bad dreams."

"Me too. What about?"

"*Romeo and Juliet*, of all things." I yawned again.

His mouth hung open. "Seriously? Me too!"

"That's weird. I wonder why?"

"Probably because you've been talking about callbacks and rehearsals a lot." Benny pushed his hipster glasses back up the bridge of his nose.

"Are you saying I talk too much about theatre stuff?"

"Maybe you just talk too much in general."

I cuffed him on the side of the head. He pushed me and laughed.

The bell rang.

"Uh oh!" I ran to my classroom, but had just enough time to shove him as I jetted away.

Chapter 8

The sun had begun to make its descent. The chill in the air hinted at a brisk fall evening. On my way to rehearsal, my phone rang. I looked in the rearview mirror. Shoot. A Mercer Island cop car was behind me. They would for sure bust me if I answered it while driving, and I didn't have Bluetooth in this old car. I pulled over to the side of the road, watching the cop drive past me.

I answered the call. It was Mike.

"Hi, Jenny. It's me."

"Hey, you!" I pictured his dreamy face, that lean, muscular body, his green eyes...

"What are you up to?"

"Just going to rehearsal. What about you?"

"In between loads in the dorm's laundry room."

"Sounds fascinating." I laughed. "I bet you're missing home already."

"No, my mom trained me well. I've been doing my own laundry for years."

"Good for her."

"Listen, I didn't call you to talk about laundry. I actually called because I wanted to know if you want to go out this weekend."

"Oh, sure, yeah," I said.

"Any place you'd like to go?"

"Surprise me."

He laughed. "Okay. How 'bout if I pick you up Friday night at six-thirty?"

"Sounds good."

"See you soon. Bye, Jenny."

I felt giddy. Another date with Mike. I turned on my blinker, looked in the rearview mirror, and... what was that? A dark smoky shape had appeared in the mirror. I blinked. It was gone.

I rubbed my eyes carefully, trying not to smear my makeup. I guess I had stayed up a little too late the night before. I pulled back onto the road, hoping I wouldn't be late for rehearsal.

***

"I'd like you all to meet Anthony Jones," Jack, our director said. "He is a professional fight choreographer."

The boys grinned and elbowed each other.

"He's going to teach those of you who will be in the fight scenes to sword fight."

Anthony came up on stage with a long, hard-case box. He undid the clasps and pulled out a sword. "You probably think these are fake. They're not."

The girls gasped. The guys were practically salivating.

"Is he serious?" I whispered to Madeline. "The last thing we need is to give high school boys sharp weapons. Geesh."

"The only difference," Anthony continued, "is that these swords have been blunted. So, while they are real steel, they are not sharp."

I watched one guy's face crumple in disappointment.

"However, they're still very dangerous. You can do all kinds of damage, even with a blunt instrument. If I see you screwin' around and swiping at each other in between scenes, you're out of the show. Understood?"

Holy moly. He was serious. A hush fell over the boys.

"Now then." Jack stepped out toward the edge of the stage. "I'd like to have everyone who is involved in the opening fight scene to stay here with Anthony. The rest of you can go to the Blue Room with Miguel and work on the other scenes."

***

We took a little over two hours running several scenes. I was standing, script-in-hand, when the door to the Blue Room opened. It was Jack.

"Ready to join us on the main stage? We'll show you what we've done with the fight scene, and then we'll add in your scene after that."

"Do you think they were able to control themselves?" Madeline asked as we walked down the hall and into the lobby.

"I don't know." I stopped to take a sip from the water fountain. "Guess we'll find out."

The guys were waiting on stage, their anticipation palpable.

"Let's take it from the top of the fight." Jack sat down in one of the audience seats. We followed his cue and sat down as well.

"No, sir, I do not bite my thumb at you sir, but I bite my thumb, sir." The boy who played Sampson bit his thumb, his eyes sparking with the challenge.

The guy who played Gregory stepped forward. "Do you quarrel, sir?"

The Abraham character responded. "Quarrel, sir, no sir!"

Their banter went back and forth. I could feel the energy of their eagerness to fight. The room was electric.

"Draw if you be men. Gregory, remember thy swashing blow."

44

Swords raised, the fighting began. I held my breath. Something felt wrong. I looked to the faces of my peers, all intently staring at the flashing of blades.

The clanging of the metal grew louder. I glanced at Anthony. His eyes narrowed as he watched. "Hey, guys, take it easy. Not so aggressive."

But instead of toning it down, they kicked it up a notch. A shorter guy in the middle of the action stepped forward, his blade nicking a taller boy's hand. A tiny trickle of blood dripped onto the stage. The shorter guy looked astonished, like he couldn't believe his sword had done that.

"Stop!" Jack roared. "Drop your swords. Now."

"What the hell is going on?" Anthony said, his voice full of venom. "What did we spend a better part of an hour talking about?"

The actors on stage looked dumbfounded.

"Safety," Anthony spat. "Clearly, you didn't hear a word I said."

I wrapped my arms around myself. A chill ran up my spine.

"They are in so much trouble," Madeline whispered.

"Tomorrow," Jack said quietly to the boys, "we are going to have a very long discussion on safety. I would hate to have to notify your parents of your behavior. This is serious, people. You cannot let this happen again, do you understand?" He crossed his arms and glared at the motley crew.

The color had drained from their faces. The actor who had drew blood bit his lip and looked down at his shoes.

"You are all dismissed." Jack turned and walked through the double doors into the lobby.

"Holy crap," a girl behind me said. "That was intense."

I grabbed Madeline's arm. "Something really weird is going on here."

Chapter 9

After rehearsal, I sat in the kitchen, eating ice cream. Mom had picked up Mukilteo Mudd and Island Coconut from the store on the way home from work. I swirled the two flavors together in my bowl.

"It was so weird, Mom." I licked my spoon. "Something was totally going on at the theatre. It's like people couldn't control their emotions. They got way out of hand. It was freaky."

"But, don't drama people get kind of carried away as par for the course? That doesn't seem too unusual to me."

"No, they really don't get that carried away. They listen to what the directors tell them to do. You just don't mess around much at theatre—otherwise you wouldn't have time to run all the scenes," I said. "Besides, the directors get pissed if we goof around."

Mom shrugged. "I can understand boys getting carried away with sword fighting, though."

"You didn't see it … the look in their eyes as they were fighting. It was almost like they were possessed."

"Now *you're* being overly dramatic." Mom laughed. "You probably don't know what to do with yourself now that there are no missing persons to find. Maybe you're looking for another mystery to solve."

"Mom." I stood up from the kitchen stool. "I'm not imagining things or making things up. I really think there is something weird going on." I put my bowl in the sink a little too forcefully, and it made a loud clanking noise as it hit the basin.

"Now, Jenny, don't be mad. I was just suggesting that maybe this isn't as big of a deal as you're making it out to be."

I suppressed the urge to roll my eyes. "Okay, fine." I left the kitchen and went upstairs to my room. Why wasn't she taking this more seriously? Maybe she was just relieved there was no mass murderer coming after me. She was probably hoping that I'd go back to being a normal teenager who only had normal everyday problems like having too few followers on social media.

But I'd learned something about myself over the course of a year. I was no ordinary teenager … and I wasn't likely to ever have ordinary difficulties. It had taken me a while to come to terms with that, but I had finally accepted myself for who I was. Sort of.

I plopped down on my bed and sighed. My phone buzzed. I looked at the screen. It was Ty.

"Hi, beautiful."

Oh my God.

"Hi, handsome."

Was I flirting?

"Did you hear Cass and me are coming to visit?"

"Yup."

"Can you spend time with us?"

"Of course! How long are you staying?"

"Tuesday thru Saturday."

"Cool. How are you?"

"Better. Hard getting over River's death. But better now."

I thought back to when he told me that he couldn't be in a relationship until he had time to grieve. That had been difficult to hear, but now I was fine with that.

"Can't wait to see you."

47

"Me too."

What about Mike? If both Ty and Mike wanted a relationship with me, I didn't know what I would do.

"Gotta go, Ty. Homework."

"Bye."

I thought of that raven tattoo, and those big brown eyes, and how his arms flexed when he was carving a totem pole. Ugh! I had to stop thinking about him. I had homework to do. And there was Mike...

One thing I hated was when girls couldn't make up their minds about which guy they liked. It was that whole *Twilight* Team Edward or Team Jacob thing. And here I was, doing the very thing I didn't like. That was not going to be me. If I couldn't decide between the two, I was better off not choosing either one.

My phone buzzed. Uh oh. Would it be Mike or Ty?

A text from cbrj84.

"Who were you talking to?"

"Who is this?"

"You know who it is."

"No, I don't."

"An admirer."

What? Who was this person?

"You look nice today."

"Thanks?"

"You are pretty."

"I don't know you."

"How can you say that?"

"Still don't know who you are. Not playing this game with you. Bye."

"I'll always be with you."

The hair on the back of my neck stood up. I shivered. I opened up my contacts in my phone. And there was cbrj84. Who the hell was this?

Chapter 10

The rest of the week went by without a hitch. School was ramping up, with the teachers giving out more homework. Rehearsals were going well. The boys had pulled it together with their fight scene, and there was no more bloodshed.

With no Friday rehearsals, I headed to the mall after school with Benny. My second date with Mike was in a few short hours, and I was anxious to talk the situation over with my pal. We sat down at a table in the food court.

"So, let me understand this," Benny scooted his chair closer and leaned forward. "You have another date with Mike tonight."

"Yes." I tucked my hair behind my ears.

"And you got a flirty text from Ty last night… and he's coming here on a college visit soon."

"That's right."

"And you got a weird text from some stalker boy who says he'll always be with you?"

"Yup."

"Damn, Jenny. I wish I had your problems!" Benny leaned back in his chair and appraised me. "I guess, if I were straight, I'd probably hit on you too."

I swatted his arm. "Stop it. I honestly don't know what to do."

"I know exactly what you should do," he said.

"You do?" I sat up taller in my chair.

"Yeah. Enjoy every minute of it." Benny grinned.

I rolled my eyes. "That is not helpful. But seriously, what do I do if Ty asks me out. What if he goes to the University of Washington next year? What if I go there next year and they're *both* there?" I started to sweat just thinking about it. "Maybe I shouldn't even apply to college there. I need to stick to schools on the East Coast. What do you think, Julliard? NYU has a great theatre program too."

Benny let me ramble on for a bit, and then put his hand on my arm. "Calm down. You have jumped way ahead of the situation. You don't know that Ty will ask you out. And you also don't know if he'll go to the U-Dub. There are too many what-ifs to worry about."

"But, Benny, so much could go wrong." A great idea popped into my head. "Ooooh, I know! You're psychic too. You can tell me what's going to happen. Use your power. What should I do?" I stared at him intently.

"Whoa there, sister, I don't know about that. You're too close a friend. You know how this works. It's harder to see someone's future if they are close to you. Besides, you know just as well as I do that psychics don't tell people what they should do. They tell them things that might happen, but the future is not set in stone. It's malleable."

"But..." I felt let down. I was so sure he could give me the solution to my problem.

"When you think about it," Benny said. "We're all like chess pieces. We move around the board, but we have to consider the other players. You might have planned your next move, but what if the other player does something unexpected? What the other person does will affect your next move. You may have to change direction. You know what I mean?"

I stared at him blankly. "Sounds like something Celine would say. But what does that have to do with Mike and Ty?"

"They're the other players. Sometimes it's smarter to wait for them to make a move before you make yours."

I sighed. "So, you're saying to not do anything until they move their pawns?"

Benny took another sip of his drink. "I'm just saying, there is no need to get all worked up."

"How did you get so wise all of a sudden?"

A wry smile crossed his face. "Because I'm the man."

"Yeah, you're the man." I patted his hand.

"Now, what you really have to be worried about is this stalker dude. Any ideas about who it is?"

The thought jarred me out of my Mike versus Ty panic. "I don't have a clue. It has to be some high school guy who has a crush on me, right?"

Benny shrugged. "I have no idea. Maybe this guy has the wrong number and got you confused with someone else?"

"That could be. I guess I won't worry about it too much. He seems harmless."

"Just be careful. Try to make sure that no one is following you. Maybe you can scan through your social media friends to see if there are any weirdos on your list."

Crap. It could be anybody.

***

Mike picked me up at six-thirty. He was wearing a blue button down shirt and dark slim-cut jeans. The blue of his shirt somehow made his eyes appear even greener.

"You are gorgeous," he said as helped me into his car.

"I was just thinking the same thing about you." I gave him a shy look.

The corner of his mouth drew up in his crooked smile. He shut my car door. Moments later he was in the driver's seat, and we headed down the road.

I smoothed down my fitted red dress and adjusted my cardigan around my shoulders.

Mike glanced at me and then shifted his eyes back to the road. "I thought we'd go do the art walk in downtown Seattle. Maybe get a bite to eat before we check out the art. Are you okay with that?"

"That seems awfully sophisticated for two teenagers," I said. Ugh. Why did I say that? "I mean, that sounds really cool, but I'm not sure I'm in the mood to go on an art walk." I looked down at my heels. "Not to mention, these shoes weren't meant for walking."

"Oh, I'm sorry." He furrowed his brows. "Would you rather go out to a movie or something?"

"No, that's okay, I was only kidding." I had embarrassed him. "We can do the art walk if you want. Or, how about if we go to a play?"

"A play, huh. That's a good idea. Do you know what's playing at any of the theatres?"

I pulled my phone out of my purse and brought up the Seattle Times arts section. "*Anything Goes* is playing at the 5th Avenue Theatre. I'd love to see it."

"Sounds like a plan." Mike took the on-ramp to I-90. "We can get a quick bite to eat at the pizza place across the street."

***

We were next in line at the ticket booth.

"Two, please." Mike got out his wallet.

"I just had some really great seats open up in the orchestra level," the woman at the counter said.

"Let's go Dutch." I opened my purse. I knew how expensive orchestra level seating was.

"You're students, right? Today, there's a student special today—only twenty bucks a seat, but I'll need to see your student IDs."

I smiled gratefully at the woman and got out my identification card. She looked at them and handed them back.

"Okay, you're all set." She handed us our tickets.

Mike pushed my money away as I tried handing him a twenty. "Really, it's not a problem. I asked you out."

I didn't say anything, but let him pay.

Walking into the theatre made me giddy. Even though I had been here many times with my parents, it never ceased to take my breath away. The inside was lavishly ornate, like the inside of the most beautiful jewel box you could imagine. The colors were all red and gold; every detail intricate and well-designed.

Mike took my arm and led me to our seats. "Wow, the box office lady was right. These are great seats."

We were only six rows from the stage. The lights dimmed, and the orchestra played the overture. I nudged Mike, and our eyes met. This was absolutely magical.

The heavy red velvet curtains opened. I held my breath and couldn't wait for the show to begin. Icy cold tendrils curled down my arm. The air conditioning must have kicked in. Mike noticed me shivering and leaned into my arm. He reached for my hand—his touch felt like a glacier. "Oh!" he whispered in alarm. "Your hand is freezing."

I frowned. "No, *your* hand is freezing." I pulled it away from him and rubbed my hands together. Strange. I shivered and crossed my arms over my chest. Could there be a vent on the floor between our seats?

The first scene began; the set looking like the top of a large ship. Sailors swabbed the deck, and passengers stood around chatting.

My purse vibrated. I had forgotten to turn off my cell phone. I reached in and pulled it out. A text message—from cbrj84. *"You're mine,"* it read. I gasped. I glanced over my shoulder. Had this guy followed me to the theatre? My heart galloped in my chest. Whoever was stalking me was here, I

53

could feel it. I turned my phone off and shoved it back in my bag.

"Anything wrong?" Mike had a concerned look on his face.

I flashed back to the end of the last school year, when the creepy guy had stabbed Mike in the chest. Mike had been trying to protect me. I couldn't let anything like that happen again.

"No. Everything's fine," I whispered.

Chapter 11

The next day, Benny and I sat in the Newcastle Starbucks sipping our lattes.

Benny leaned forward. "So, the guy texted you? How did he even get into your contacts list?"

"I don't know. I certainly didn't put him in there." I stared at my phone. "He's also sent me an Instagram notification—but with no picture. Just a black square."

"That's bizarre." Benny wiped up a spill next to his cup. "But you think he followed you to the 5th Avenue Theatre?"

"Yeah, how else would he know that Mike had reached over to hold my hand? I mean, it was at that *very* moment that my cell phone went off."

"Sure is a mystery. Between the two of us, though, we should be able to figure this out. We're psychics for cripe's sake." Benny's one eyebrow shot up, making me laugh. I nearly shot coffee out my nose.

"What?" He looked at me innocently.

"Heh, it's that…" I pointed to my eyebrow. "You know, that thing you do with your…"

"I don't know what you're talking about." He barely masked his grin.

"Anyway, I guess I'm pretty rattled about this guy."

"How do you know it's a guy?" He raised his other eyebrow up.

"Stop it!" I giggled. "But I guess you're right. I don't know that it's a guy. The energy around it seems so masculine though. I just assumed."

"*She* could be a very masculine lesbian," he suggested with a totally straight face.

I rolled my eyes. "Now you've gone too far."

"I'm serious. It could be anybody. We shouldn't make any assumptions."

I glanced at my phone again. "Oh, shoot! It's twelve forty-five. I don't want to be late to rehearsal."

We got up and pushed our chairs in.

"Just watch your back," he warned. "Be hyper-aware. This kind of person is probably a total whack job." Benny opened the door for me, and we stepped onto the sidewalk. He grabbed my hand and looked at me intently. "Promise me you'll be careful."

"Okay, I promise."

***

Madeline and I waited outside by the entrance to the theatre. We were early. The sun had finally started to burn off the thick layer of clouds overhead.

"Julia said that she saw you and Mike in downtown Seattle yesterday. Are you guys back together?" Madeline pulled her hair back into a pony tail and secured it with a hair tie.

"Oh, I didn't realize Julia had seen us."

"Yeah, she and Aya were going to a movie downtown. She said they honked at you, but you didn't see them."

I shrugged. "There's a lot of honking downtown. I didn't realize it was for us."

"So, are you?"

"Back together? Um, sort of. We're starting all over again—but really slowly this time. The last thing I want to do is jump into a serious relationship right now."

"But you guys are perfect for each other! Why wouldn't you want a serious relationship?"

I bit my lip. I could list a million reasons. For one thing, I didn't want to get hurt. What if Mike decided that I would be too much of a distraction from his freshman year of college again? Then, there was the fact that I didn't know where I would be going to college myself. If I ended up going to New York, I wouldn't see Mike for a long time. And then there was Ty. I had no idea what to think about that situation.

"It's complicated."

"Well, for the record, I think you two make the perfect couple." Madeline checked the time on her phone. "Where is everybody? Rehearsal starts in five minutes."

Cars began pulling into the parking lot. Most of the people in the play had their driver's licenses, but there were a few that were being dropped off by their parents. Soon, we were surrounded by hugging teenagers and the sound of their chatter echoed off the theatre's exterior walls.

Miguel, the stage manager, opened the doors to the lobby. "What are you all doing out there? Come on in, we're waiting for you."

***

After rehearsal, the sun had gone down. The air had taken on a definite edge; the crisp air foreshadowing the impending autumn.

"Do you need a ride?" I asked Madeline.

"No, I drove here. Dad finally broke down and got me a car." She pointed at the charcoal gray Corolla.

"Nice!"

Caleb came up behind us and tapped me on the shoulder.

"Agh!" I shouted.

Madeline cracked up.

"Sorry, Jenny. I didn't mean to scare you." Caleb's face turned red. "I was just going to ask if I could bother you for a ride. My dad is out of town, and my mom just put my little brother to bed, so she can't leave the house."

"Oh, sure." I put my hand on my heart to calm my nerves. "Where do you live?"

"Down at the south end of the island. I hope it's not too far out of your way."

"No, that's fine, Caleb." I turned to hug Madeline. "See you tomorrow."

We got into my car and pulled out of the parking lot.

"Sorry, I don't know my way around Mercer Island much. How do I get to the south end?"

"You take a left on Island Crest Way and keep going for several miles. I'll let you know where to turn."

The night was black, and even blacker on the road we headed down. Trees flanked both sides of the street, and only an occasional street light brightened the evening. The silence was awkward. I felt like I should fill it somehow.

"How many brothers and sisters do you have?" I asked.

"Two. One of each." Caleb looked at me shyly. "I'm the oldest. How about you?"

"I just have one little brother. He's eleven and just started the sixth grade."

Another awkward silence. Why did this feel like a blind date?

I cleared my throat. "So, you're a junior?"

"A sophomore. And you?"

"I'm a senior. I go to Newport." I glanced at him. "I'm assuming you go to Mercer Island High School?"

"Yup."

We approached a four-way stop sign.

"Take the next road after the intersection." Caleb pointed.

More silence.

I wondered why he was acting so strangely. Was he afraid of me?

"Uh, listen, Jenny. Would you like to go out sometime?"

Oh. So that was why he was nervous. I had to give the kid credit. He had the balls to ask out a girl two years older than him.

"You mean, just you and me… on a date?"

His face, which had already been red, went crimson now. "Okay, I know that seems weird, but I thought since we are supposed to have chemistry as Romeo and Juliet, and we don't know each other all that well yet, that we could, you know, maybe go out for dinner and a movie or something like that. To, you know, break the ice, and stuff."

Oh my God. "Caleb, that's a great idea, and you're a super nice guy, but…"

He looked out the window. "But the answer is no, right?"

"The thing is, I'm two years older than you. I'm kind of seeing someone right now, and…We can hang out in a group if you want. That might help with the chemistry thing." I put my hand on his arm.

Flash.

I'm so confused. I like her, but I've never liked a girl before. The last crush I had was on a guy. Now I've made a fool of myself. How can I ever look at her again?

"Let's hang out tomorrow." Poor guy; he just needed to figure out who he was. "I'll ask Madeline and some of the other people from the cast if they want to come to my house. We can make cookies and watch a movie. What do you think?"

He sighed. "You sure? I mean, if it makes you uncomfortable…"

"Nope, it doesn't at all. I'd love to hang out with you."

A slight smile brightened his face. "Yeah, I'd like that. That's my house—on the right."

I stopped at the curb, and he jumped out.

"See you later!" I waved, but he had already turned away.

***

Back in my room, I turned on my laptop while I changed into my t-shirt and pajama pants. As soon as I sat down, a window popped open on my monitor. Ty was asking to Skype me. I held my breath. I wasn't sure if I should say yes. I had just sort of agreed to start dating Mike again.

But Ty was a friend. I couldn't just turn him away. I accepted the call.

I knew the second I had clicked the button that I should've ignored him. Those gorgeous brown eyes—and the dimples. God, I was a sucker for dimples.

"Hey!" His smile lit up my screen.

"Hi, Ty." I was glad he couldn't see my hands fidgeting. Why was I so nervous?

"How have you been?"

"Pretty good. And you?" What was with the small talk? I felt like an idiot. I had to attempt a substantive conversation.

"Is everything all right with your mom and your family? I'm so sorry about your cousin—I know how close you two were. But I'm glad we found her, you know. I mean, I'm sorry she didn't make it, but at least now she can be at peace." I must've had brain damage. Why was I talking about this?

"We're all doing okay, under the circumstances." The smile left his face.

Wow, good job, Jenny. Now I had dredged up some depressing memories. "Crap. I'm sorry, Ty. I shouldn't have brought it up."

"Not a problem. My family and I are just getting through each day the best that we can." He brushed the hair out of his eyes.

"So…" I looked down at my lap, feeling self-conscious.

"Actually, I just wanted to call and see you. I miss you."

"Oh. I miss you too." I smiled at him, thinking that this already awkward conversation was about to get more awkward. I contemplated telling him about Mike.

"I told you we are coming down to visit the University of Washington, right?"

"Uh-huh."

"Maybe we can hang out together, the three of us, that is."

A good sign. He wanted to hang out with me *and* Cassandra. I didn't have to tell him about Mike, because he probably didn't like me that way anymore. Okay, I could handle this.

"Sure! Yeah, that sounds like fun. I'll bring Benny with me."

"Good. I'm looking forward to it."

Silence. "Okay, see you." My mouse hovered over the red off button.

"Jenny?"

My finger stopped short of the click. "Yes?"

"You look beautiful."

And just like that, my heart skipped a beat.

Chapter 12

"Thanks for letting me invite the cast over to our house, Mom." I grabbed an apple out of the fridge and took a bite.

"Not a problem. But tell me again, why are we doing this?"

I explained about Caleb and how he asked me out. "It was awkward, you know? He said he wanted to get to know me better so our chemistry would be better on stage. Instead, I suggested that we all hang out as a group at my house."

"Good plan." Mom sipped her coffee. "Then he won't feel rejected, and the whole cast can bond."

"Exactly."

"What time are they coming over?"

"At four o'clock. I figured that would give us time to clean the house before they arrive."

"Us?" Mom put her hand on her hip.

I gave her a sheepish grin. "Yeah, I thought we could do it together."

"You're forgetting, I have to run to the grocery store to buy food. You'll have a mutiny on your hands if you don't provide dinner and snacks for a houseful of teenagers."

"Oh, yeah, I didn't even think about food." I groaned. This was turning into a lot of work.

"Take it from me, before you invite people over, you need to think the whole thing through."

"Sorry." I hated it when adults were practical. It took the joy out of everything.

She jingled the car keys in her pocket. "I'll be back in a couple of hours. Good luck with the housework."

Great. Now who was going to help me clean? My phone buzzed. It was Benny.

"Want to go to the mall and hang out?"

"How about if you come over here?" I had a diabolical idea. "Can you stay for dinner?"

"Sure. What time should I come over?"

"As soon as you can."

***

"This was not part of the agreement," Benny said as he mopped the kitchen floor. "You said you wanted me to come over to hang out."

"We are hanging out." I wiped down the countertops with a rag. "We're just multi-tasking; hanging out and getting stuff done. This is quality time."

"Since when is *cleaning* quality time?" He said "cleaning" like it was a dirty word.

"Benny," I said wrapping my arm around his shoulders. "Any time I spend with you is quality time. You're the best."

He rolled his eyes. "Whatever. Why are you making me do this?"

"Because I'm having the cast over for a get-together. I'd like you to meet them."

"There's more to this than you're telling me." He looked me straight in the eye. "Spill it."

I sighed. "Damn your psychic ability." I told him about Caleb.

"So, you read his mind—he likes you, but he's confused that he likes you, because the last person he liked was a dude?"

63

"Yup."

"So, he's bi?"

I shrugged. "I guess so. Maybe he's just confused about his sexuality and hasn't decided yet. I don't know."

"I'm not sure I want to stay for dinner." Benny wrung the mop out in the sink.

"Why not?"

"For starters, I won't know anyone but you and Madeline." Benny looked over his shoulder at me. "Sometimes, I feel awkward in a group of strangers. What if they don't like me because I'm gay?"

I stared blankly at him. "Seriously, Benny? These are *theatre* kids."

"Oh, well, you've got a point there. Okay, I'll stay. But if I get any judgmental vibes, I'm out of here."

"Fair enough."

***

Mom had gone all out and made grilled chicken, roasted baby potatoes, and a Caesar salad. The garlic bread had just come out of the oven and lay steaming on the bread board.

"I think you're salivating a little," I joked.

Benny made some loud slurping noises and pretended to attack the bread.

"See that? That's drama. You'll fit right in with the cast."

The doorbell rang. The first guest had arrived.

I walked into the living room and opened the front door. Benny followed close behind.

"Caleb! You're the first one here!" I almost hugged him, but realized that wasn't a good idea.

"No, I don't think so." He looked behind me and glanced at Benny. "Is this your boyfriend?"

64

Benny's eyes got really big and then he laughed. "Me? Oh yeah. Jenny's my girl all right." He grabbed me from behind and planted a kiss on my neck.

"Knock it off!" I swatted him away.

Did I detect jealousy in Caleb's eyes?

"Caleb, this is my best friend, Benny. I thought it would be nice if he could meet the cast—since I'm constantly talking about you guys. At least now he'll know who everyone is."

"Oh." Caleb reached his hand out politely and shook Benny's hand. "Nice to meet you."

My friend must have gotten some kind of psychic impression from Caleb. He looked startled for a moment and then let go of Caleb's hand.

The doorbell rang again. Madeline and a group of five more teens had arrived, and more were walking up the driveway.

"What is that delicious smell?" A guy named Ari stepped through the door. "Is that for us?"

"My mom made us dinner. Go ahead into the dining room," I said, pointing the way.

Whatever Benny had learned from the handshake would have to wait until later.

***

I popped the DVD into the player. "I rented *Romeo and Juliet*." We were lounging in the living room, sprawled out on the couch, recliners, and floor.

"The Leonardo DiCaprio version?" Sydney asked.

"No, I got the Franco Zeffirelli version from 1968."

"Too bad," Ellie said. "I kind of like Leonardo's portrayal of Romeo."

"Let's not lie," said Griffin. "What she's really trying to say is that she likes Leonardo's ass."

"Ha ha." Ellie threw a pillow at him. "I heard there's nudity in this version too."

"That's okay, it's art." Sydney laughed.

I got up and dimmed the lights. As I stood in the darkened room, I felt everyone's energy. They were all happy. Benny was sitting between Caleb and Madeline, laughing at Sydney's smart remark. He fit in so well with this group of kids. My eyes wandered back to Caleb. There was a strange energy pulsing in him. Quiet energy, but different than that of the other people.

Goosebumps rose on my arms. Despite the fact that I was wearing a long-sleeved shirt and a hoodie, I was suddenly chilled.

Chapter 13

After the movie was over and everyone had gone home, I helped Mom clean up the kitchen.

"Thanks for letting me have the party." I placed the last cup into the dishwasher.

"You're welcome." She put the leftovers in the fridge. "Seems like a nice bunch of kids."

"Yeah, they are."

"How did the thing with Caleb work out? Do you think he still likes you?"

I shrugged. "Maybe. I don't know. It's odd—I'm getting a strange vibe from him, but I can't quite figure it out."

"Huh. Like a bad vibe?"

"No, I don't think so. His energy—I'm getting mixed signals from him. It throws me off. I don't know where he's coming from. Know what I mean?"

Mom looked pensive for a moment. "Yes, I think I do. Some people are just like that."

"Do you still get visions? I know you said that you were sort of psychic when you were young, but it scared you. You did the same thing I tried to do—you pushed it away."

"Funny that you asked me that. Remember when you told Dad and me about your gift? It was in the hospital, after Richard Grist shot at you."

I nodded.

"Ever since then, I've been more aware. You know?"
She chewed on her fingernail. "Kind of like, I just *know*
when something will happen."

"Maybe it's because you're accepting it a little more,"
I said.

"Could be."

"Does it still scare you?"

"No, not really. I've actually learned a lot from
watching you."

"You have?"

"Yes—you're kind of like my psychic role model."

"Oh, brother." I giggled and hugged her. "Well, I'm
going up to bed."

"Okay, honey, sleep well."

***

Once I was ready for bed, I snuggled down into the
covers and thought about what my mother had said. It was
nice that she was accepting her gift too. I turned over onto
my side and drifted off.

"Jack and Diane" blared at full volume on the radio.

*The blond boy sitting in the back of the car with me was
singing loud enough to be heard over the stereo. He took a
swig of his beer.*

*"You know this part about life goes on? Do you ever
wonder what happens if life doesn't go on?" he asked me.*

"Huh?"

"If the thrill of livin' is gone, what's the point?"

*The guy in the driver's seat turned around to look at us.
"Hey, Joe Philosopher back there, drink your beer and shut
up. We're trying to listen to the music. I love this song,
man." He fiddled with the dial and turned the volume up
even higher.*

*I resisted the urge to cover my ears. The blond boy
winked at me. "Let's talk about this later."*

68

I woke up, my ears still ringing with the music. Because most of my dreams actually meant something, and were linked to some kind of crime, I knew I was in for another mystery. But why would I have a dream about some random people I didn't even recognize? Closing my eyes, I tried to recall the blond boy sitting in the back seat of the car with me. Was he somebody from my school? I shook my head. He didn't look familiar at all.

My alarm clock glowed green on my bedside table. Three o'clock. I groaned. Waking up in the middle of the night sucked. I rolled out of bed and put on my slippers. The house was chilly. I pattered down the stairs and into the kitchen.

To my surprise, the light was on.

"Mom?"

She was sitting at the table, her hands wrapped around a steaming cup of tea. "Jenny, you startled me."

"Sorry. What are you doing up?" I took a mug out of the cupboard and set it on the counter.

"I could ask the same of you," she answered.

"A dream woke me up. Then I started thinking about it and couldn't go back to sleep."

Mom's eyebrows arched. "I had a dream too. That's why I'm down here."

I put a tea bag in my cup and poured in some hot water. "What was it about?"

Mom sighed. "That's just the thing—I have no idea. It didn't make any sense."

"Welcome to my world," I muttered, plopping down in the chair next to her.

"All I saw was a boy arguing with his mother, but I couldn't hear what they were saying. I saw their mouths moving, and they were gesturing with their hands. I could tell by the looks on their faces that they were angry with one another."

"Did you recognize them?" I took a sip of my tea.

She shook her head.

I told her about my dream.

"That doesn't make any sense either. Weird." Mom got up and put her empty mug in the dishwasher. "We really should go back to bed."

"But what about figuring out what the dreams mean?" I asked.

She sighed. "I guess we'll have to wait until we have another dream to find out."

Chapter 14

The conservatory classes for *42nd Street* were scheduled for Fridays at four o'clock. This was the first class in a string of many before the real rehearsals began. After school, I had driven to the dance store to get some new tap shoes. My old ones were at least a size too small and had killed my toes during callbacks. That left me with just enough time to run home, change clothes, and wolf down some leftovers.

Mom walked in just as I was leaving. She was wearing her power suit—a sure sign that she'd had a presentation at work.

"Bye, Mom!" I yelled as I slung my dance bag over my shoulder. "See you later."

"Where are you going? I thought *Romeo and Juliet* rehearsals were only Monday through Thursday."

"And Saturdays," I reminded her. "But I'm going to the *42nd Street* conservatory class tonight."

"Oh, yeah." She looked frazzled. "I'm having a lot of trouble keeping you and your brother's schedules straight this year."

"Next year will be a lot easier for you." I adjusted the strap on my bag.

"It will? Why?"

"Because I will be away at college—so you only have to worry about Jackson's schedule."

Her face fell. "Right. But I'd rather have two kids to fuss over." She brushed her hair behind her ear. "I can't believe this is the last year you'll be living at home."

I rushed over and hugged her. "Oh, Mom, it's not like I'm leaving forever. I'll just be gone from September through June. And I'll be home for Thanksgiving, Christmas, and spring break."

She wiped a tear from her cheek and laughed. "All right, I know. I just don't like thinking about you leaving, that's all. I'll miss you."

"It's going to be okay. See you tonight." I closed the door gently behind me. Poor Mom. She was going to be stuck all alone in the house with Jackson and Dad. All that male energy. Ugh.

***

Sweat trickled down the girls' faces.

"Again!" Lea, the choreographer shouted. "And one, two, three, four, five, six, seven, eight."

Finally, the music stopped. The cast flopped down on the floor.

"Pretty good," she said. "Let's take a break."

I felt bad for all of them. Because I was playing the part of Dorothy, the veteran actress who couldn't actually dance all that well, I didn't have to work up a sweat. I grabbed my snack and a bottle of water out of my bag and sat against the wall.

"How did we look?" Mara, the girl who played the lead role of Peggy sat down next to me.

"Great!" I took a sip of my water. "Especially you— you must have a lot of dance training. Did you even break a sweat?"

She laughed and opened a bag of chips. "Yeah, of course I did. Can't you tell?" She wiped her forehead and

72

feigned exhaustion. Her hair was tied up in a loose ponytail. I admired her dark skin and thick curls.

"I used to dance," I said. "And I was a cheerleader. It's kind of sad that Dorothy doesn't get to dance much in this show. I feel kind of jealous of you all."

Mara crunched her chips and swallowed. "Well, just be glad you get to sit out. Even though I'm a dancer, she's kicking our butts. I'm beat." She glanced at Lea, who was talking to the music director by the piano.

The hair on my arms stood up. "God, it's October. You'd think they would turn down the air conditioning in here." I rubbed my arms.

"Huh, I'm not cold." Mara gave me a sideways glance. "Besides, this part of the building doesn't even have air conditioning. Maybe it's because I was dancing and you weren't."

"Probably."

More people joined us on the floor. Just as we got comfortable and fell into easy conversation, the music started up again.

Jan sat at the piano and waved us over. "Come on, we're going to learn another song."

***

After rehearsal, I went straight home. Jackson was sitting at the kitchen table flipping through a cookbook.

I felt his forehead. "Are you sick?"

He brushed my hand away. "No. I'm looking for a recipe for chocolate chip cookies."

"You're going to make cookies?" I was completely floored. Jackson had never shown interest in cooking or baking before. He would be happy to go to fast food restaurants for every meal—and Krispy Kreme donuts were his idea of the perfect dessert. "Did you ask Mom for help?"

"She's not here; she's helping a friend move into a new apartment."

"And you can't wait for her to come back?"

He shrugged. "Sometimes you just need a good chocolate chip cookie, you know?"

I smiled. "Yeah, I know. Want me to help you? We can make them together."

His face brightened. "Really? You would do that?"

"Why not? Heck, I could use a good chocolate chip cookie myself."

"Is this recipe okay?" He pointed to a page in the cookbook.

"Looks good to me. Come on, let's get out all the stuff."

***

The cookies were out of the oven, and Jackson and I stood at the counter eating one after the other and chasing them down with glasses of ice cold milk.

"That was actually kind of fun!" He licked the chocolate off his lips.

The door leading to the garage opened, and Mom whisked into the room. She was wearing old jeans and a stained sweatshirt. Her eyes bulged when she saw Jackson and me together.

"Did I just walk into the wrong house?"

Jackson and I looked at each other and cracked up.

"I mean, seriously," Mom said. "You guys made cookies… together?"

"What's the big deal?" Jackson took another bite of his cookie.

Mom shook her head. "I'm just astounded, I guess. I never thought I'd see the day."

"He's growing up." I tousled his hair. "Jackson's not so bad anymore."

My brother swatted at me, but it was a playful swat.

Mom turned around and opened the door. "Well, that does it. I've definitely entered the wrong house. I'm going back out to find my real family."

"Hey!" Jackson ran over to close the door before she could walk through it. "You have to try one of these cookies first. After all, you just helped carry a couch up two flights of stairs."

She stood motionless, her mouth hanging open, and finally reached out and took the cookie he offered her. "Uh, thank you."

I looked at my mom and then looked back at Jackson. "How did you know she carried a couch up two flights of stairs?"

He froze.

"Yeah," Mom said. "How did you know?"

"I'm not sure. It just popped into my head."

Mom and I exchanged a knowing look.

The garage door opened again. Dad came in and stopped short. He looked at the three of us and noted the looks on our faces. "What's going on here?"

"I don't think you want to know," I said.

Chapter 15

Back in my room, I yawned and stretched. I'd just finished filling out another college application. The prospect of college seemed both exciting and a little scary. Would Mike and I still be together by next fall? And what about Ty?

I huddled underneath my pile of covers and took a moment to think about the rest of the school year. I hoped I could get everything done; keep my grade point average up, do well in the theatre productions, have a social life, and manage to finish all of my college apps on time.

I was making myself crazy. I took a deep breath and looked at the clock. It was after eleven o'clock already. Sleep was necessary if I wanted to master my schedule. I groaned and rolled over to my side. Despite being stressed, I found myself slipping into a restless sleep.

The hallway was wider than the one in my school.

Students walked past me, heading toward their classes. A girl bumped into me. She had ridiculously permed hair— her bangs poofed up like a rooster comb.

"There you are." The boy from my last dream appeared in front of me. "Have you thought about what I said?" He grabbed my hands and kissed my cheek.

"I—don't know." My voice sounded meek.

"It's for us, babe. It's the only way."

The bell rang.

My eyes flew open. My alarm clock was blaring on my nightstand. I smacked the snooze button. What the hell? I pulled the blankets back over me and shivered. Something was up, but I had no idea what it was. The hallways in the dream weren't the hallways of Newport High School. Why was I dreaming about a guy I didn't know in a school that wasn't my own?

"Please, God, don't drag me into another mystery," I thought. I had too much to do. Couldn't I just have a normal senior year? The alarm went off again. I sat up and turned it off. A new feeling of unease crept into the pit of my stomach.

***

It was Saturday afternoon. We had just finished the kissing scene. Caleb's eyes glimmered—he seemed more comfortable and confident with his kiss.

"Great job! I can tell you two have really worked on your chemistry." The director winked at us.

Perfect. Humiliating and concerning at the same time. Caleb obviously still liked me.

"Jack, which scene are we rehearsing next? The balcony scene?" Miguel asked.

"Yes, that's the one." Jack motioned for me to climb the ladder to the tower. "Places!"

The cast moved into their spots—most were off stage. Brrr. It was cold in here. I regretted not wearing my hoodie.

"Go ahead, Jenny." Jack pointed at me with his pen.

I cleared my throat and stepped into my light. *"O Romeo, Romeo, wherefore art thou Romeo?"* I looked down at Caleb from my turret. *"Deny thy father and refuse thy name."*

Caleb was hidden behind a bush. Really? The stage directions were silly. Wouldn't Juliet see him from up high?

Personally, I could see everything from up here, including him.

"Shall I hear more, or shall I speak at this?" Caleb asked, his head turned toward the empty auditorium.

I shivered, but continued. *"'Tis but thy name that is my enemy. Thou art thyself, though not a Montague. What's Montague? It is nor hand, nor foot, nor arm, nor face, nor any other part belonging to a man. O, be some other name!"*

The turret creaked. I shifted my feet. Shoot... what was next?

"Line!" I called out.

Miguel glanced down at his script. *"What's in a name? That which we call a rose by any other word would smell as sweet."*

"Oh, yeah." The turret creaked some more. I looked down at the platform I was standing on. It seemed to be leaning a little—and the wood made a groaning sound. I turned my head to watch a nail slowly work itself out of the wood structure. Huh?

"Do you need another line?" Miguel asked, slightly annoyed.

Should I say something? I stepped back from the railing. I was probably just being paranoid.

"Uh. No, I got it." I cleared my throat. *"Retain that dear perfection which he owes without that title. Romeo, doff thy name, and for that name, which is no part of thee take all myself."*

A loud crack sounded beneath me. Cold air skittered across the nape of my neck. What was happening?

Caleb jumped up from behind the bush. "Jenny!" He rushed toward me.

"No, Caleb! Get out of the way!" I yelled. I held onto the wrought-iron rail as the tower split apart and tilted toward the stage. I scrambled backward like a crab, trying to grab hold of anything I could. My heart pounded loudly in my chest. A girl screamed. My hands grasped at air as I tried to find something to keep me from falling.

The red velvet curtain swooshed past me. I grabbed it with one hand and held on.

Shouts rang out all around me as the tower hit the surface below. I swung toward a board which had separated from the main structure. A sharp pain raked my arm. I saw the gleam of a nail poking out from the wood. Blood erupted from my skin and ran in a warm rivulet down my arm.

"Catch her!" a girl shrieked. "She's going to fall!"

Caleb reached me first and grabbed a hold of my legs. "It's okay, I've got you."

But Jack and Miguel pushed him out of the way and lowered me to the stage.

"Your arm," Caleb gasped.

"Ugh," I croaked, the shock of the accident muddling my thoughts.

"Go get Katie," Jack barked at Caleb. "Tell her to bring the first aid kit. Miguel—call Jenny's mom. Tell her she needs to go the emergency room—she may need stitches… and a tetanus shot."

That last comment did me in. My vision blurred, and the lights went out.

Chapter 16

"You've got to stop getting yourself involved in these crazy fiascos," Dad said, taking a sip of his coffee. "I am a little tired of getting these emergency room bills."

We were sitting at the breakfast table the next morning. The bandage wrapped snugly around my arm peeked out from my long-sleeved hoodie. I ate a bite of my cereal and stared at him. "Really? I didn't get myself into this. It was an accident."

"Are you sure it's not related to some psychic thing?"

"Come on, Peter, Jenny is just doing a normal play. It's not like the last two times—when she took it upon herself to find two missing people. Or three, if you count River…" Mom's voice trailed off, and she self-consciously brushed the crumbs off the table.

Anger welled up inside me. "You know what, Dad?" I stood up from the table and grabbed my bowl. "I don't know why the tower fell to the stage, but I didn't intend for that to happen. It wasn't my fault. The least you could do is act supportive and concerned that I was injured."

I went into the kitchen, dumped my bowl into the sink a little too loudly, and came back to the dining area to continue the argument.

Mom gave me a sympathetic look and then glared at Dad. "She can't help it, you know."

Dad looked exasperated, and I swear he would've made a comment about women, but my brother walked into the room.

"At last," my father said, "someone who speaks my language."

Jackson rubbed his eyes. "I had this really weird dream last night that Dad got a flat tire."

Dad's face paled. He pushed away from the table and opened the door to the garage, flinging it ajar with a whoosh. A few seconds went by. "Damn it!" he shouted.

Mom and I looked at each other, barely containing amused smiles.

He reappeared in the doorway, his face red. "This place is a nuthouse."

We all turned to look at Jackson.

"What?" he said.

***

I was savoring my last few hours of Sunday. I had finished my homework, and was stretched out on the family room couch watching trash TV. This was the best part of the week—when I had absolutely nothing to do.

My phone buzzed on the coffee table. I reached over and grabbed it—probably just Benny. It was a text from cbrj84. Who was this person? I rubbed my eyes and looked at the screen.

"I like a girl in red," the text read.

I sat bolt upright. "What the hell?" I looked down at what I was wearing… the red shirt I had recently bought. Somebody was watching me. My heart started beating faster. I got up and looked out the window. Nobody. Panic welled up inside my chest. I hadn't been outside all day. How would anyone know what I was wearing?

I hurriedly closed the blinds and sat back on the couch. A fleece blanket was draped over the back. I gathered it around myself. I didn't know what to think. I stared at my cell phone screen, waiting for another text to appear, but there was nothing.

**

"You might need to alert the police," Benny said as we sat at the cafeteria table the next day.

I snorted. "What am I going to say, 'I've been receiving strange text messages from someone I don't know'? Right, me and five million other teens... it doesn't constitute a crime. The police can't do anything about weirdos unless they actually harm someone. Don't you watch *Law and Order?*"

Benny shrugged. "What about Detective Coalfield? You guys are still in touch, right?"

"I occasionally see him at the grocery store, but other than that, no."

"Maybe you'll just have to catch the creep in the act then."

"Like, put up surveillance cameras around my house?" I took a bite of a soggy French fry.

"Not a bad idea," he said.

"I suppose..."

The bell rang. We picked up our trays and dumped them in the receptacles.

"See you later. Do you need a ride home after school?" I reached out and adjusted Benny's hipster glasses.

"Sure." He waved and disappeared into the crowd of students.

My phone buzzed. I bit my lip and pulled it out of my pocket.

"He's not for you." The text read. Again, it was from cbrj84. I whirled around. The stalker was here! Students streamed past me on either side. I tried looking for anyone who had their phones out—but they all had them out, most

82

were texting and walking. This was like looking for a needle in a haystack.

Frustrated, I jammed my phone in my pocket and headed toward my next class.

***

"Let's recap," Benny said. He was sitting in the passenger seat of my car with a notebook and pencil. "Tell me all the places and times you've received texts from this cbrj84 person."

I stopped at the light. "Hmmm… let me think. I got a couple at home, one at YTN, and one at school. I got one when I was with Mike at the 5th Avenue Theatre too."

"It sounds like this person is definitely following you, or just knows how to creep you out at the right time."

"He doesn't necessarily have to be following me. Maybe he knows where I'm going and with whom and then sends the texts after he knows I'm there or something. I don't know. It's really scary."

"I'll give you that."

We reached Benny's drab brown house. I pulled over to the curb. The yard was a little overgrown and sad-looking. The dirty white paint was peeling off the front door. Benny's parents weren't much into keeping up appearances. I glanced around at the other houses on the block. Most were nicely kept, with fresh beauty bark snuggled up to azaleas and rhododendron bushes.

Benny stood awkwardly on the sidewalk, hugging his messenger bag to his side. "Want to come in?"

"I'd love to, but I've got to get home and eat before rehearsal tonight."

He looked relieved. "Okay, thanks for the ride."

"Sure." I waved and pulled out into the street.

My phone buzzed. I caught a glimpse of the message as it lit up my screen. "Stay away from him," the text read. It was from cbrj84.

Chapter 17

By the time I arrived at Youth Theatre Northwest, I was completely creeped out. I was certain there was someone or *something* there that didn't like me. I was sure a ghost hadn't caused the tower to fall—that was probably just an accident. Besides, I didn't think they could do that. However, the idea that there could be some kind of entity there was unnerving me.

Not only was the ghostie creeping me out, but now I was on full alert because of the phone stalker. This person seemed to know what I was wearing and who I was with most of the time. I found myself constantly looking over my shoulder and jumping at the slightest sounds.

I opened the doors to the lobby, and nearly shrieked. Someone had come up from behind and tapped me on the shoulder. I whirled around, only to see Benny's grinning face.

"Benny!" I shoved him back. "What the hell? You scared me to death." My heart was pounding a million miles an hour.

"Surprise," he said sheepishly. His face bore the look of guilt and amusement. "I signed up to tech for your show."

I put my hand over my heart. "Good God. I think I need to sit down." Thankfully, the bench in the lobby was only a few feet away.

Benny sat down next to me, and slung his arm around my shoulders. "Hey, I'm sorry I scared you. I just wanted it to be a surprise."

I nodded. "I'm sorry I over-reacted. How did you get here anyway? I just dropped you off at your house."

"My dad let me borrow his truck."

"The one with the gun rack?" I smiled.

"Yeah, I know. But it's better than nothing."

"For sure." I took a deep breath. "I'm glad you're here. Let me know if you get any indication that there's a ghost here. Some strange stuff has been going on."

"Okay."

Students started to trickle into the lobby. The volume of their banter filled the room. Theatre kids did not know how to use their inside voices.

Miguel opened the doors to the main stage. "Come on in, gang."

Benny stood up and stuck out his hand. "Hi, I'm here to do the light board."

Miguel grasped his hand and shook it. "Oh, good. Glad you could do this."

We walked into the theatre. Miguel showed Benny to the booth in the back, and the rest of us sat down in the auditorium seats.

Jack was talking with the lighting designer and caught a glimpse of me. He excused himself and approached me. "Jenny, are you doing okay? How's your arm?"

I rolled up my sleeve to show him the bandage. "It's much better, thanks." I glanced up to where the tower was. It was back up again, and reinforced with a metal frame.

Jack followed my gaze. "You don't have to worry about that happening again. The technical director made sure of it."

My shoulders relaxed. "Honestly, I was terrified to go up there tonight."

Madeline came in and sat down next to me. "Looks like they fixed it." She tipped her chin toward the tower.

"Yup. Let's hope they bolted that sucker down."

"Attention, everyone!" Jack called to us. He was standing up on stage. We're going to work on the first scene, but I'm going to send small groups over to the costume designer for measurements. Madeline, Caleb, Jenny, and Ross, why don't you go first?"

***

We stood in the hall between the lobby and the smaller studio stage. The costume designer waited for us next to the open door to the costume closet. The middle-aged woman with a pair of chained reading glasses perched on the end of her nose appraised us.

"I'm Helen. Let me see—let's take you first." She pointed to Madeline and rolled out her measuring tape. "Tell me your name and your character's name." She scratched down Madeline's information on her chart.

Caleb and Ross looked mildly uncomfortable as the woman measured Madeline's waist, chest, and arm span. I sat down on the floor and waited patiently.

When it was my turn, Caleb reached out to pull me up. His hand lingered on mine a little too long.

I cleared my throat and told her my name and character name, expecting her to jot it down.

"Ah, Juliet. I have just the dress, and by the looks of you, it should fit perfectly." She grabbed my arm and tugged me into the costume room.

The small space was tight and packed with garments hanging from racks. "Wait just a moment," she said. "I have to go up to get it."

A ladder was tucked in on the left side of the doorway. My eyes followed her up the narrow wooden steps. I hadn't

87

realized that there were another two tiers of costumes hanging straight above the ground level.

"Ah! Here it is," she called from up high.

Cold air seeped into the room. I shivered and looked around nervously. Icy tendrils tickled my neck.

"It's cold in here," Helen mumbled, her voice muffled by the volume of fabric. "Be a dear and take this from me." She leaned over, reaching the long dress down the steps.

The hangers began to rattle.

"Don't shake the ladder!" Helen said with alarm.

"I'm not." I answered. Fear surged through me. "I think you better come down here. Quick."

"What?"

The rattling increased. Now the floor trembled as well.

"Earthquake!" Helen screeched.

Costumes fell off the wire hangers onto the floor. From high above, clothes flew out in all directions and landed in a heap at my feet.

The floor shook more violently. Helen careened from side to side on the platform above. She reached for something to hold onto, but she grabbed only costumes, which immediately came loose and tumbled down.

A cold hiss blew into my ear. *"Die."*

My heart pounded. I tried to steady myself as the floor shook.

Above me, Helen sounded like a frantic chicken, disturbed from her nest. "Oh, God. An earthquake, an earthquake!"

"Hold on, I'm coming up to get you." I grabbed hold of the sides of the wooden ladder and stepped up one step, and then another two steps.

The costumer screamed when the shaking became even more violent. I watched in horror as she lost her balance completely and fell through the opening. Whump! We lay in a heap on a pile of clothes below, Helen on top of me.

"What the hell?" Ross stuck his head in the closet.

The rattling stopped.

A dress was covering the side of my face, but at least my left eye was uncovered, and I could see out.

Madeline and Caleb's heads appeared in the doorway next to Ross.

I tried talking, but the wind had been knocked out of me, and Helen's slightly overweight form was not making it any easier.

"Jenny?" Madeline stepped in and started pulling costumes off of Helen and me. "Are you under there?"

Helen began whimpering.

"Oh!" Madeline said when she yanked the last dress off of us. "Oh my God."

"Madeline, come out of there so Ross and I can get in," Caleb said.

The boys entered and helped Helen off of me, then pulled me up on my feet. Neither one of us was hurt, but Helen was a basket case.

"Why did I let my husband talk me into moving to Seattle? He's perfectly aware I'm terrified of earthquakes. And why did I get a job on Mercer Island for God's sake? Everyone knows it sits right on top of a fault line. Honestly, what I was thinking?"

Ross looked confused. "Earthquake?"

"Yes, an earthquake." Helen scrutinized his face for signs of mischief. "Oh, come on now. Don't tell me you didn't feel that."

My friends shook their heads.

"What?" Helen put her hand over her heart. "I'd say it was at least a 7.0."

"No, we really didn't feel anything. Not a thing," Ross said.

"But that's impossible." Helen thrust out her arm dramatically. "Just look at what it did." A majority of the costumes were pooled on the floor.

"Huh," Caleb grunted. "That's very odd, but we didn't feel any shaking out here in the hall."

My friends were looking at Helen like she was a complete nut job. I remembered back to what the old Jenny was like—the one who was in denial of her ability. The old Jenny might've thrown Helen under the bus and pretended she was crazy. But I was the new Jenny—the girl who tried to help people with her gift whenever possible. And Helen didn't deserve that.

"What Helen said is true. The entire closet was shaking. It really did feel like there was an earthquake in there."

Helen looked relieved.

Ross looked skeptical. "Seriously?"

Madeline could see by the look on my face that something supernatural was going on.

"Does this have anything to do with…"

"Yes," I interrupted. "I know you are going to think I'm crazy, but there is a ghost in this theatre."

Helen gasped. "A ghost! Are you sure it's not an earthquake?"

I looked at the boys, who seemed to be on the verge of either laughing or being scared.

"Yes, I'm sure. You guys swear you didn't feel the ground shaking, right?"

Madeline shook her head. "But we heard stuff fall off the hangers, so—how would a ghost make everything shake in there?"

I shrugged. "Don't know. I've never experienced anything like that." I turned to look at Helen, who had tears pooling up in her eyes. "Have you ever seen anything strange or had any weird things happen while working here?"

"No, no. I just started this job last week. Nothing out of the ordinary has happened." She smoothed down her skirt. "Besides, I don't believe in ghosts. Everyone knows there's no such thing."

Madeline and I exchanged a glance. I turned my attention to the guys. "How about you two? Have you seen or heard anything weird lately?"

"Well, there are rumors about the YTN ghost, but I've never seen anything. Last year, one of the boys in the cast of *The Hobbit* swore he saw a dark shape coming out of the boys' dressing room," Caleb said.

Ross snorted. "I'm with Helen. Ghosts are just a myth—like leprechauns and unicorns."

I hesitated. I wanted to say something about my own personal experience with Michelle, the ghost that haunted Newport High School. She was no longer there; I had helped her move on to the other side. The new Jenny should volunteer this information. But there was just enough of the old Jenny left that I held my tongue.

Chapter 18

I needed to find out what to do about this ghost. Clearly it was an angry ghost. But why? Not knowing anything about these kinds of things, I decided to call the one person I knew who did—Celine.

She had been my mentor for all things psychic ever since the second half of my junior year, when I'd worked with Detective Coalfield to find a missing girl from my school.

My body was still trembling from the incident at the theatre, so I climbed onto my bed, fluffed up my pillows, and wrapped myself in an extra blanket.

I skimmed through my contacts list, found Celine, and called her.

"Hello, Jenny," her voice chimed. "Is everything all right?"

"No, not really." I explained about what happened in the costume room. "And the weird thing is no one outside the room felt anything. Inside the closet, it was like a major earthquake."

"Did you get any indication that the ghost was there before the shaking started?"

"Yeah, sort of. I felt cold on my neck and around my shoulders."

She paused. "What kind of impressions are you getting from the ghost?"

"Only that it intends to hurt me. I mean, I think it made the tower crash to the stage too."

"Tower?"

"For *Romeo and Juliet*. I play Juliet. I was in the middle of my soliloquy—you know, 'Romeo, Romeo, wherefore art thou Romeo?' when I felt some cold air around me. The wood made a creaking noise and before I knew it, the tower was falling."

"Has this ghost tried hurting anyone else?"

"No, I don't think so." I pulled my blanket around me tightly. "I don't get why this thing seems to hate me."

"Try talking to it," she said.

I hesitated. I really didn't want to engage in a conversation with this thing. "I guess. What should I say?"

"Tell the ghost that it needs to move on to the other side; that it has died here in this reality, but there is something better waiting for it in the light."

My head was filled with doubts. I wasn't so sure the ghost would listen to reason. "I'll give it a shot…"

"Try that first. Let me know how it goes. If that approach doesn't help, give me a call."

"All right, thank you, Celine." I ended the call. I chewed on my lip. What if it didn't work? What if the ghost tried to kill me again?

My head was pounding, and my eyelids felt heavy. I crawled under the covers and pulled them up to my chin. I just wanted all of this to go away.

We were at Skate King, holding hands. Eye of the Tiger was blaring out from the speakers. I watched as poofy-haired girls skated nimbly past us.

"Let's get married," the blond guy said.

"Married? But we're only seventeen—we're too young," I said.

He pulled me off the rink and leaned me against the wall. "But we're in love." He brushed the hair off my face. "We can drop out of school and start our life together."

"What? No, I want to finish school. And I want to go to college too. You're only saying this because you can't stand living with your parents."

His face turned red. "Are you saying you don't love me?" He pressed me harder against the wall.

"No, that's not what I'm saying." I swallowed hard. He was on the edge of explosive anger again. How was I going to calm him down? "Sure, I'll marry you. But let's take some time to plan this, okay?"

He backed off a little. "There now—that's all I wanted to hear. We'll get married. Take some time to plan it, but I don't want to wait too long. And no matter what, we'll be together." He drew me closer and whispered into my ear, "Forever."

I woke up and shivered. It was the same guy from those other dreams I had. My heart was still pounding.

***

Breakfast was peanut butter toast. I sat, sipping my tea at the kitchen table. My head hurt from a night of restless sleep.

"Hurry up, or you'll miss the bus!" Mom shoved a sack lunch into Jackson's hands. "And don't forget, I'm picking you up early to take you to your dentist appointment this afternoon."

"Yeah, yeah." Jackson opened the door just as the bus squealed to a stop.

Mom looked at me. "Why aren't you out the door already?"

"I hit snooze one too many times." I yawned. My stomach was still twisted in knots. "Had some weird dreams that kept me up all night."

"Were they those vision-y dreams?" Mom poured herself a cup of coffee and joined me at the table. Her brows were furrowed as she studied my tired face.

"Yeah, and most of them seem to take place in the 80s."

"The 1980s?" Mom looked surprised.

"I have no idea who these people were or what they have to do with me. It's so bizarre."

Mom shrugged. "Maybe it doesn't mean anything at all."

Having had many paranormal experiences in the last year, I highly doubted it.

Chapter 19

It was after school on Tuesday, and I was relieved I wasn't scheduled for rehearsal. Thankfully, only the people who were in the fight scenes were called. I plopped down on the couch and planned to vegetate in front of the TV for an hour or two before digging into my homework.

My mind was cluttered with thoughts of bad dreams, scary texts, closet earthquakes, and falling towers. All I wanted was to *not* think.

I brought up Netflix and scrolled through the lists of movies and shows. I shuddered as scary show after scary show zipped by. *The Shining, The Killing, American Horror Story, The Walking Dead.*

I scooted back into the cushions, yanked the blanket off the back of the couch, and pulled it over me. God, was it horror week or something? Then I remembered. Halloween was coming up at the end of the month. Ugh.

Thankfully, I found a mindless romantic comedy and relaxed. Not thinking was good.

It was so warm and comfy under the blanket. My eyelids drooped and I stifled a yawn. It wouldn't hurt to rest my eyes for just a few minutes.

"Mrs. Babcock, your son has had many infractions here at school, and it's not just this one I'm concerned about," the man with the glasses said. His hair was wispy

on top, making his skin seem even more sallow in the fluorescent light.

"I'll have a talk with him." I shifted uncomfortably in the hard chair.

He sighed. "I don't think you understand, Mrs. Babcock. It's beyond having a talk with him."

I glared at him, wondering why he was being so unreasonable.

"Look," his voice hardened, "He's violent. I don't know what's going on at home, but your son is troubled."

"What do you mean?" I was alarmed. "Are you accusing me of abusing him or something?"

"I didn't say that. But his behavior is erratic. I'm afraid we can't deal with that sort of thing. It's too dangerous for the rest of the students to have him here." He pushed his glasses back up the bridge of his nose.

"So, what are you saying? Are you suspending him again? Surely, what he did wasn't that bad..."

"No, I'm not talking about suspension. I'm talking about expulsion."

"What? Don't do that. Please. I don't know what else to do with him. I've tried to—"

He stood up. "I'm sorry. Your son needs professional help, and we can't risk the safety of his classmates having him at school. As of today, your son is expelled."

I put my hands over my face and sobbed.

"Jenny?" Mom was shaking me.

My eyes flew open. "Wha?" I was curled up in a ball on the couch, my face wet with hot tears.

"Honey, what's wrong?" Mom hovered over me. She knelt down and stroked my hair. "Did you have another bad dream?"

I took a deep breath and nodded.

"Care to tell me about it?"

I hugged myself and shivered. "More stupid dreams that don't make any sense to me." I told her what I saw, not even knowing who the people were.

Mom joined me on the couch and put her arm around me. "Do you suppose you're seeing the mother of the boy you've been dreaming about? The one who seems so hateful toward his girlfriend?"

Why hadn't I thought of that? She was right. That must be his mom. This guy was out of control. But I still had no idea why I was dreaming about someone from the 1980s. Or his mother, for that matter.

"You've had dreams about his mother too."

"Yes," Mom said. "I believe I have. I've had dreams of a mother arguing with her son. I can't see their faces, and I don't know if it's the same mother and son from your dreams."

There was one thing I knew for sure, I needed to figure this out soon, or I would be having these damn nightmares for a long time to come.

***

I barely got through school on Friday. I was so tired from trying to fit in homework and after school rehearsals that I was ready for the week to be done.

Unfortunately, I had to attend my conservatory class for *42nd Street* at the theatre after school.

After I arrived in the blue room, I sat down on the floor and put on my tap shoes, trying to psych myself into having the energy to dance. Even though my role wasn't heavy on tapping, I was learning the dances anyway. It had paid off last week, when I was able to step in for one of the chorus girls when she was out sick.

The choreographer, Lea, cleared her throat. "We're starting at the top of 'We're in the Money.' Places!"

Fifteen minutes later, everyone was drenched in sweat. Especially the girl who played the lead character.

"You're an amazing dancer," I told Mara. "How long have you been tapping?"

She swiped the back of her hand over her forehead. "Since I was really little."

"Makes me want to take up lessons again."

"Let's do that one more time." Lea clapped her hands.

Mara took a swig of water and took her place in the center of the group.

I wasn't in this number, so I sat with my back against the wall to watch.

"One, two, three, four, five, six, seven, eight!" Lea called.

The music of the piano filled the room.

Next to me, the door opened, and a group of men stood there with measuring tapes and clipboards. "Oh, sorry," one of them said. He closed the door.

They had let in a draft. I shivered and wrapped my arms around me.

Mara bounced across the room with the rest of the dancers, looking woozy. Her character, Peggy Sawyer, was a dancer who had just moved to New York City and had not yet earned any money. She was dizzy from hunger.

The guy who played Julian Marsh, the gruff director of the tap show, walked onto the floor. Peggy Sawyer was supposed to bump into a row of chorus girls and fall.

But when Mara bumped into the other dancers, she fell for real. It was almost as if she flew across the floor.

I held my breath and watched in horror as she came down hard.

Mara shrieked.

Lea and the Director, Meg, dashed to her side. "What happened?"

"My ankle!" Mara sobbed. "I think it's broken."

Lea's face drained of color. "Susan," she said to the stage manager, "Get some ice. And call Mara's mom. She needs to go to the hospital."

When Mara had been picked up, Meg and Lea took me into the hall. "Jenny, I don't want to freak you out, but I don't think Mara can play Peggy Sawyer if her ankle is broken," Meg said.

"But rehearsals don't start for another month," I said. "That's enough time for Mara to heal, right?"

Lea and Meg exchanged a glance.

"When you break a bone, you have to rest it and then build your strength back up," Lea explained. "There's no way she can tap on it, even after it's healed a while."

"So, what are you saying?"

"Lea is saying the only way we can make this work, is for you and Mara to switch roles. She can be Dorothy—who has virtually no dance scenes, and you can be Peggy." Meg put her hand on my shoulder.

I let out a heavy sigh. "But I can't dance like Mara can."

"Maybe not," Lea said gently. "But you've had dance training—and that's more than the other girls in the cast. It's got to be you."

I was doubtful. Could I really pull this off? But if there was no one else… "I guess I can do it."

"Good. I may have to call a few additional rehearsals for you so we can work on the more difficult steps." Meg studied my face.

I swallowed. I felt the hairs stand up on the back of my neck. Just what I needed. More time in this haunted theatre.

Chapter 20

Halloween snuck up on me without much warning.

I hadn't even remembered to buy a costume. Benny, Madeline, and I were sitting in my family room, watching Stephen King's *Carrie*. We had just gotten to the part where Carrie stood on stage after she was crowned prom queen, when the bucket of blood was dumped on her from above. I covered my eyes while the blood ran down her face. Blech.

Benny paused the movie. "Are you okay? You look a bit pale."

Madeline got up off the couch. "Should I go get our snacks from the kitchen?"

I rubbed my stomach. "Maybe a little later."

We sat in silence for a few moments.

Madeline cleared her throat. "Isn't there some sort of Halloween thing at YTN?"

"What thing?" Benny turned off the TV.

"They're doing a haunted theatre. It's kind of like a haunted house, but there's an actual story behind it."

"Is it super scary?" I was still getting over the sight of blood. I wasn't sure I wanted to get grossed out at a haunted house.

"No, not really." Madeline sat back down.

"Sounds fun." Benny slung his arm around my shoulder. "I think we should go."

I glanced out the window. It was almost dark. Soon the trick-or-treaters would be banging on the door, demanding candy. "Yeah, let's go."

Fifteen minutes later, we arrived in the theatre's lobby. It was adorned with cobwebs, crooked paintings, and an old chandelier hanging from the ceiling. The crystal pendants dangling off it caught the yellow glow of the lanterns placed on the tables and floor.

I shivered. "Well, this looks sufficiently creepy."

"You're scared already? They haven't even begun the show yet," Benny said.

I elbowed him and gave him a sour look.

Miguel came through the double doors leading to the theatre. He was wearing a dark red, velvet suit and what looked like a bell-hop's hat. "Welcome," he said with an old-fashioned 1930s-type inflection. "Tickets may be purchased here." He pointed to the ticket booth, where a woman dressed in a long, gold gown sat with a cash box.

When we'd gotten our tickets, Miguel showed us through the double doors into the theatre.

"Please, have a seat." He went back out into the lobby to bring in more guests.

"Do we know anyone in the show?" I asked Madeline.

"Yeah, Ross and Caleb are in it. And a couple other guys from *Romeo and Juliet*, I think."

More theatre-goers entered the theatre auditorium and took their seats until we had an audience of about fifteen people.

"Sad that there aren't many people here." I looked behind me at the sparse turn-out.

"Oh, this is full for a show like this. They run every thirty minutes or so, and we won't be sitting here the whole time."

"What?" Benny seemed taken aback. "Where else will we be?"

"They take us all over the theatre—down hallways, into other rooms… So, they really can't have a large number of people. The ones in the back of the line wouldn't be able to hear or see what was going on."

The lights went down and a spotlight shone on stage. Ross came out wearing a brown, tweed suit with his hair slicked back. Tinny music began playing softly from what sounded like a gramophone.

"Ah," he said. "I see you're all here then." He nodded to us. "Thank you for coming. I'm so glad I won't have to face this night alone."

The sound of thunder boomed in the auditorium. The spotlight flickered.

Ross gave a nervous laugh. "You see, you're here to help me find the little boy—find him before his soul is lost forever."

I shifted uncomfortably in my seat.

"This grand theatre has been standing for over eighty years." Ross motioned to our surroundings. "But the time has come when it will be torn down. A rich businessman is demolishing the theatre and is planning to build a multi-story high-rise on this very property."

"More like, the school district is tearing down the theatre to build an elementary school," a person behind me whispered.

"As I mentioned before, there is a little boy who needs your help. He must be found before the theatre is destroyed—or his soul will be lost. Forever."

A girl sitting in the front row with us raised her hand. I could tell she was part of the production. "Excuse me. What happened to the little boy?"

Ross nodded at her. "I'm glad you asked, Miss. Let me show you." He stepped to the side of the stage and motioned toward the center of it. The spotlight went out and the lights came up.

"The year was 1932. Just two years after the theatre was built."

A small boy and a teen boy and girl dressed in formal "parent" clothing stepped into the center of the stage. Their clothes were all gray, like a black and white movie.

"But Papa, can we please go see the show playing at the theatre?" the little boy pleaded.

The father was irritated. "No, we cannot. I've told you, there's something strange going on in that theatre. It wasn't built properly from the very beginning. I believe it's dangerous. Not to mention that I've heard about some— strange activity happening there."

The mother smoothed the boy's hair down. "I'm sorry, James, but your father is right. Why, just the other day, Velma Goodwin told me that she'd gone to see a show and something grabbed her ankle from underneath one of the seats."

Just then, Madeline let out a bloodcurdling shriek, causing my heart to stop dead in my chest.

Some of the audience members screamed too.

"Something grabbed my ankle!" Madeline shouted.

We all realized at once that this was part of the show. People laughed, and everyone quieted down again, wondering what would happen next. I patted Madeline's arm and relaxed. So, this was how it was going to be, eh? I wouldn't let some silly scare-tactics get to me tonight. This would be fun.

"Mother, Velma is always making things up." The boy pouted. "The other day, she said she thought Mr. Johnson from the post office was possessed by the devil."

James' father chuckled. "Well, Velma does have a tendency to stretch the truth when she drinks."

"Although, she might have a point there," James' mother said. "Mr. Johnson certainly does look a tad bit pale."

Shadowy bats appeared on the back wall of the stage and fluttered off-stage.

I snorted and clapped my hand over my mouth. This was campy, not scary.

"It's your bedtime, anyway," the father continued. "Off you go."

The lights went down, and some props were pushed on stage. When the lights came back up, James was in his little bed, wearing pajamas.

"Good night, James!" his mother called from off-stage.

"Good night, Mother." James got out of bed and unbuttoned his pajamas. Underneath, he was wearing a dark shirt and pants. He lit the lantern by the bedside.

"Now I can go explore the theatre," he whispered. "And I'll be back by dawn. Mother and Father will never have to know." He climbed out the window.

The lights went out and Ross reappeared on stage in his spotlight. "But, you see, his mother and father *did* find out. Because the next morning..."

The man and woman walked out on stage.

"James, time to wake up," his mother said.

"James?" His father pulled back the covers.

A look of horror crossed their faces and the lights went out.

When the lights came back up again, Ross was standing back on stage. "James' parents were distraught. Search parties were deployed and they scoured every inch within miles of their home. To no avail. James was simply... gone."

The little girl in the audience raised her hand again.

"Yes, Miss?" Ross pointed to her. "Do you have a question?"

"Did they search the old theatre?" she asked.

"Why, yes, they did." He looked out at the audience. "But they only searched during the day. And we all know how old buildings like this change when the sun goes down, and shadows fall between every nook and cranny."

Another clap of thunder reverberated through the theatre.

"Finally, I have assembled a group of people brave enough to search this theatre late into the evening. You." He pointed to us. "I bid you—search every alcove, behind every door and cobweb. I feel certain that James is here…somewhere. Find him before this building is torn down. Find him before his soul is lost forever."

A lightning bolt flashed across the stage, and the theatre rocked with the sound of thunder accompanying the flash. Ross was gone, and we were left in the dark.

When the dimmed audience lights were turned on, a girl about my age was standing before us, wearing a gold blazer with a name tag that said, "Lara – Official Tour Guide." Her skin was exceptionally pale, and her stage makeup enhanced the dark circles under her eyes.

"Please, follow me." She held up a lantern, turned, and walked toward the auditorium doors, which opened with a creak before we reached them.

Lara stopped in the lobby and beckoned for us to gather around her. "Stay close to me. Do not wander away from the lantern's light. There are… things… lurking in this old theatre that I have no name for. Strange things. Some are benign. Some are not."

A shiver ran down my spine. Benny nudged me and grinned.

"We will systematically search the building. We don't have much time. This is the last night the theatre will be standing. James's soul is depending on you. Don't fail him."

She held the lantern up and walked to the left side of the lobby. A heavy door with a solid brass doorknob stood next to the closed doors of the registrar's office. Lara brushed the cobwebs away from the door. She took out a gold key and clicked it into the lock.

"First, we'll search the costumer's sewing room."

We followed Lara into the dark interior. She shone the lantern on the short flight of stairs that immediately greeted us as the door swung open. Cobwebs were thick along the walls of the staircase. We timidly followed her up each step.

She stopped halfway up on the landing. "Watch out for rats."

Just as she spoke, shadows of rats scattering every which way appeared on the sides of the stairs. A few shrieks pierced the narrow entrance, but there were many more laughs and giggles than fearful sounds from our group.

"How did they rig up a projector in this tight space?" Madeline whispered at my side.

Something in my peripheral vision caught my eye. A real rat scurried out from under a prop left on the stairs and darted out the open door. I screamed, which set off most other people in our group.

"Shhhh," Lara whispered. "If James is here, you don't want to scare him away." She continued up the stairs.

We emerged at the top and tried to squeeze into the loft-like space. Lara lifted her light to reveal the room.

A long table, with a couple of sewing machines perched at either end, was positioned in the middle of the space. Plastic tubs filled with fabric, thread, and other sewing accoutrements were nearly bursting from every area available—under the table, along the walls, and tucked into corners.

Our guide clutched the lantern to her chest, where it eerily lit her face from below. "Search this room well. He could be hiding anywhere."

I swallowed. I knew this tale wasn't real, but I couldn't stop the trickle of fear that began gurgling in the pit of my stomach.

The group broke up and began looking under the table and behind boxes. There was another door toward the back.

I caught Benny and Madeline's gaze and nodded my chin toward it. "Let's look in there," I whispered.

We wound our way through the others until we reached the door.

"Ready?" Benny had his hand on the knob.

"Go ahead." Madeline stepped back a little.

He turned the knob and pushed it open.

"Raaaaaawwwwwwwrrrrr!" A girl, dressed all in white and wearing white makeup threw herself at us. "Who dares to disturb my peace? Get out!" Her piercing screech made my heart stop.

Our entire group erupted into panicked shouts. We thundered down the stairs in total blackness, stumbling over each other as we tore down the steps.

Once we were safely back in the lobby, I turned to Madeline with an accusatory glare. "You said this wasn't very scary."

She looked down at her shoes. "It wasn't scary last year."

"Yeah, well, they have upped the fright factor in a big way," I grumbled.

Benny was loving it. "This is totally awesome." He grabbed my arm. "Come on, let's see what's next."

My insides were like jello, and my stomach had begun to feel unsteady. I reluctantly followed behind him.

Madeline scooted up beside me. "I can't figure this out. You don't seem scared when you're dealing with kidnappers, bad guys with guns, and paranormal phenomena. But you're scared of a fake haunted theatre?"

Maybe she was right. It did seem silly for me to be scared of a staged production. But I knew this theatre truly *was* haunted. And I knew that the real ghost, whom I had encountered one too many times, was systematically trying to kill me.

I frowned at her. "It's not the fake haunted part I'm scared of."

Realization crossed her face. "Oh. I guess I get it. But, it should be fine. There are lots of other people here. Surely the ghost wouldn't try anything with all these, uh, witnesses around."

"He had no problem 'trying anything' while he made the tower, with me in it, crash to the stage."

Her cheeks reddened, and she sighed. "You're right. Sorry."

God. What was wrong with me? I didn't need to bite my friend's head off. She and Benny were just trying to have some Halloween fun. Why did I have to be such a downer?

I blew out a breath. "No, I'm the one who should be sorry. This is supposed to be spooky and fun. I'm sorry I'm so jumpy and irritable."

"Quickly," Lara said. She had already gone halfway down the back hallway. "Please don't linger behind. There are dangers here."

I tried to smile. "Come on, we'd better catch up with the rest of the group."

***

I was certain we had overturned every prop, costume, and chunk of wood in this place, all the while being accosted by various dead-looking characters in scary costumes. When we finally reached the Studio Stage black box, the small theatre space in the back of the building, my senses had numbed to the constant assaults.

"This is our last chance," Lara said. "If we don't find James here, his soul will be forever lost. He'll never join his long-dead parents, who crossed over to the other side decades ago, and have been waiting to reunite with him ever since he disappeared."

Too damn bad. My nerves were on edge and I was done looking for this kid.

We followed our guide through the doorway of the black box, trailing behind the rest of the group.

"I feel James' presence somewhere in this room," Lara whispered. "Look for him."

The audience scattered in the dark, lantern-lit room, looking behind the stage curtains and in dark corners.

"Check this out," Benny motioned toward a door at the back of the stage. "He's probably in here."

Madeline and I huddled close to Benny, expecting to see a little boy actor waiting to be discovered.

Benny turned the door knob gently. The lock clicked and the door creaked open a few inches.

Suddenly, a dark shadow in the form of a person swooshed out of the room and loomed over us. We stepped back, wondering how the production crew could've created such a spectacle.

But when the shadow swirled and formed into human shape, I knew this was no special effects magic. This was the real deal. I was too shocked to scream, and I could tell by the look on my friends' faces that they knew it too.

The dark smoky shape formed into the figure of a young man wearing a Romeo costume. His face was contorted with malice, and he raised a dagger in his clenched fist.

We backed up in horror.

The rest of the audience saw the ghost too, but they thought it was part of the show. A few people pointed and laughed. "How did they do that?" I heard one person say.

The ghost swirled around us, its form breaking up in movement, but coming back together when it stopped.

I grabbed Benny and Madeline's hands. "We've got to get out of here!"

"You don't have to tell me twice," Madeline squeaked, and we turned and ran.

We bolted for the door, but the ghost swooshed past us with frightening speed and blocked the doorway. I caught a glimpse of the emergency exit toward the back of the room. "This way!"

All three of us spun on our heels and ran toward the glowing green exit sign.

The dark shape was right behind us. I turned to look over my shoulder, but tripped over Benny. I came down on my hands and knees and looked up in time to see the mass of darkness cloud over me. The ghost took form and raised his dagger hand. He plunged the ghostly knife deep into my chest.

Ice cut through me. I clutched my chest and took in a ragged breath. Fear paralyzed me. Yet, I was still alive. The ghost roared in anger—and then disappeared in a puff of air.

The rest of the audience members were looking on with amazement. They seemed to love the ghostly Romeo and were buzzing about how cool and scary it was.

Benny hauled me up to my feet. "Are you all right?"

I looked down at my chest. No blood, but my skin below my neckline was blue from the cold.

Lara the tour guide looked even paler than her makeup allowed. This wasn't part of the shtick, and she knew it.

"Hey, I found James!" someone shouted from behind the stage curtain. The crowd erupted in applause.

"Let's get out of here," Madeline said.

We made it to the hallway.

"That was insane." I massaged my temples with my fingertips. I felt a nasty headache coming on.

Madeline stood, shaking. "Probably the scariest Halloween I've ever had."

Even Benny looked a little shaky. "The movie we were watching at Jenny's is suddenly looking a lot more appealing. Let's beat it out of here."

"I want to forget this night ever happened," I said.

Chapter 21

"Remember that UW visit we talked about?" Mom handed me a confirmation card.

"Yeah." I had just come home from school. I took the card from her.

"Well, I scheduled it. There's the info."

I checked the date and time. "Oh, good. Thanks." Then I remembered that Cassandra and Ty were coming to visit on the same day. "Oh my God, my friends from Alaska are coming. They'll be here next week!"

I was excited, but also overwhelmed. It would be tech week at the theatre—which meant long tiring rehearsals every night and our opening night performance on Friday.

My phone buzzed. "Hello?"

"Jenny, it's Mike."

"Hi, what's up?" I left the kitchen and sat down in the quiet living room.

"Not much, but I haven't talked to you in a while—school has been so busy. I thought it might be nice to go out. I mean, would you like to go out?"

"When?"

"How about this Friday night? Dinner and a movie?"

"I can't. I have a conservatory class at the theatre." I twirled my hair. "But maybe another time. How is school?"

"Exhausting, but great. I miss you, though."

112

I smiled. He was being so sweet. Before he broke up with me during the summer, I had agonized about him going off to college—about all those new girls he would meet. But now it seemed as though he really wanted to be with me. I felt my guard coming down a little bit more.

"I miss you too. You know, I'm going to do a college visit there next week." Why did I say that? I would be with Cassandra… and Ty.

"You are? Let's definitely plan to meet for coffee after your visit." His low voice sounded so sexy.

What was I doing? I definitely did not want to have Ty meet Mike. It would be so awkward. I hesitated for too long.

"Jenny? Did you hear what I said?"

"Uh, yeah. The thing is, I will be visiting with a couple of friends, so…"

"From Newport High?"

"No, not exactly. My friends are coming down from Alaska. You know, I told you about them? Cassandra and Ty."

"Oh." His voice lost confidence. "The guy you had a summer fling with?"

"It wasn't a fling. I was upset because you broke up with me. He was upset because his cousin was missing." I cringed. "I don't expect you to understand. It's complicated."

I heard him sigh. "I get it. So, are you seeing him now?"

"No. How can I 'see' him? He lives in Alaska."

"Okay." There was a long pause. "So, do you want to go out this Friday—after your conservatory class?"

"That could work, I guess. I get out at 6:30."

"Good. I'll pick you up at the theatre." He paused again. "I just really want you to know that I want to make this work between us. I've already apologized for screwing things up, but I feel like I haven't expressed it well enough."

I bit my lip and thought about the day he told me he needed to concentrate on school, and how that meant he couldn't be in a relationship. For one instant, I relived the moment that he dumped me. An involuntary shiver made me draw my knees up to my chest. "I know you feel bad about it, Mike. We all make mistakes."

"It's a decision I will always regret... how I hurt you. It was wrong, and I'm so sorry."

The one remaining frozen part of my heart melted. He was sincere—and I knew that it meant I would let my walls down completely. He was worth it.

And then he totally surprised me.

"I love you, Jenny."

My heart lifted and buzzed with happy energy. All the sad memories faded. "Oh, Mike," I whispered. I ended the call, and sat for a while; a stupid grin plastered on my face. My phone buzzed again.

It was cbrj84. The message said, "Slut."

***

Later that evening, I called Madeline's dad. "Detective Coalfield." His voice sounded relaxed.

"Hi, it's Jenny. Hey, I'm having trouble with a stalker—he keeps threatening me and calling me names in texts."

"Yes—you mentioned him before. Are you all right?"

"I think so, but he's really scaring me. Are you able to trace him?"

"Why don't you bring your phone over to the station and we'll see what we can do."

"Okay," I said. "After school tomorrow? I have to be at rehearsal at six o'clock. Will you be around at two-thirty?"

"Actually, it would be better if you met me after your rehearsal. I'm working nights this week." There was some muffled noise in the background. "I've got to go, I have a situation here."

"Okay, see you at around nine-thirty then."

***

"This stalker guy thinks I'm a slut."

Benny and I were plopped down on my couch in the family room, eating popcorn.

"Are you?"

I threw a handful of popcorn at him. "No! Of course not. I don't know how this person would've gotten that idea about me. I'm still a virgin, for God's sake."

He looked surprised. "Really?"

My jaw dropped. "Yes. Do you have a problem with that?"

He shrugged. "No. I mean, I thought I was the only virgin at Newport High School."

I rolled my eyes. "Oh, come on, Benny. There are a lot of us out there. Wait—you're still a virgin too?"

"Do you have a problem with that?" He snorted.

"No, I just thought you might have gotten some action with your new hipster look, that's all."

"Not yet. Besides, I haven't found the right person."

"Want me to set you up with someone?" I grabbed the remote and turned on the TV.

"Probably not." He stared at the screen.

The Bachelor was on. Decked out in a tuxedo, the guy had twenty drunk girls all making goo-goo eyes at him.

"Why can't I be like that guy?"

I made a face. "Seriously? That's not even real. He's just a regular guy that they've clothed in designer-wear. And they gave him a really nice haircut. That mansion they are having the cocktail party in—that's not his. He probably lives in a one-bedroom apartment with beer cans littering the floor. This is all for show. I'm telling you, it's not real. Most rich guys are old and ugly."

A smile crept up the corners of his mouth. "You always have this way of making me feel better about myself."

115

"That's what friends are for." I scooted closer to him and hugged him. My phone buzzed on the coffee table.

My blood ran cold. The text said, "Whore."

***

"Here." I thrust my cell phone at Detective Coalfield. "See for yourself. The texts are from cbrj84. Don't ask how he got into my contacts list—I have no idea."

The detective took my phone from me and navigated to my text messages. His face wrinkled as he scrolled through my list. "You said the texts were from cbrj84?"

"Uh-huh." I sat down in the chair next to him. "The texts should be right before the messages from Benny."

I watched him continue to scroll.

He shook his head. "Nope, I don't see them."

"What?" I grabbed my phone back and looked at my phone. Messages from Benny, Mike, Julia, Madeline, Aya, and a whole bunch of kids zoomed by as my finger flicked the screen. "I don't get it! This guy has sent me multiple texts."

"I don't know what to tell you, Jenny." He sat back in his chair. "You said he texted you last night?"

"Yes." I bit my lip.

"Did you leave your phone out anywhere today? Somebody could've deleted them."

I thought hard. Had I left my phone out on a desk at school? No, it was in my pocket all day, except when Benny texted me between classes. After that, I went to rehearsal.

"Oh my God! I left my phone in the dressing room in my purse. Somebody could've taken it out and deleted the messages." It had to be someone in the play. Someone who knew what my purse looked like.

"Well, that does help to narrow it down to a select group of people. Any chance one of your cast mates has the cbrj initials in their name?"

Why hadn't I thought of that before? I worked through the list of actors in my head. Ross, Sydney, Madeline, Caleb. My breath caught in my throat.

"What?" the detective leaned in.

"Caleb. Caleb Black. CB." Oh, no.

"Okay, maybe. What about the RJ?"

R... J... Ross? No. His last name was Marley. "I don't think there is an RJ in the play."

"What else could RJ stand for?" he asked.

I shrugged.

"What play are you doing?"

"Romeo and Juliet."

His eyebrows shot up. "Really? *Romeo and Juliet.*"

No. Oh, no. RJ. CBRJ.

Chapter 22

The next day at rehearsal, I kept my phone in my pocket. I wasn't about to let it out of my sight. And I had to keep my eye on Caleb.

During the scene where Juliet appeared to be dead, I lay in my prone state and cracked one eye open to study his face. He was in a state of anguish, his face stained with the tears of sorrow over my death. I searched for a glimmer of contempt or grim anger, but found none. I only saw the torture his character was going through.

Clearly, he was a brilliant actor. His face did not betray the angry words he had texted me. *Slut. Whore.* That's what he called me. What kind of a creep would go to such lengths as to try to intimidate me into liking him? Did he think that I would change my mind because of his threats?

I was not as good of an actor as he was.

"Thus with a kiss, I die." Romeo had swallowed the poison after seeing Juliet dead in the mausoleum. Romeo, or Caleb rather, was lying next to me, his arm outstretched with the vial of poison in one hand.

The scene ended with me taking Romeo's dagger and jabbing it into my chest. I fell over Romeo's body, terrified that he would whisper something sinister in my ear. But he lay still.

"Are you all right, Jenny?" the director asked. He came up to the edge of the stage. "You seem to have lost your emotions here. You looked more distracted than distraught. And I wasn't seeing Juliet's pain."

"Um, yes. I'm sorry. I guess I got pulled out of the moment. Too many things rattling around inside my head." I sat up and smoothed down my dress.

Jack frowned. "It did seem like you were far away. Let's try this again—but really try to place yourself in Juliet's head instead of your own, okay?"

My cheeks burned. I usually didn't compromise my acting because of outside thoughts. Shoot. I couldn't let Caleb get to me. "Of course. I promise to take note and do it better next time."

We started the scene again from the beginning. Caleb gave me a sympathetic look, and reached out to squeeze my hand reassuringly before we began. I pulled my hand back. What the heck? Why was he being so nice to me? He'd spent the last few weeks trying to intimidate me into liking him. Jerk.

Jack cleared his throat. "Remember, focus on Juliet's emotions."

I snapped myself back into the scene. He leaned down to kiss me, and an icy breeze settled around us both. I shivered.

"You're not supposed to move," Jack called out. "I don't want to see you breathe or move at all—Romeo has to think you are dead."

I exhaled with force, angry with myself. "Okay, thank you."

"Start from the top again."

I tried so hard to concentrate on Juliet's emotions that I kind of over-acted my part. Disappointment made my face turn red again. I sat up. "Jack, I'm really sorry. Can we do this just one more time?"

He sighed. "Yeah, okay. Next week is tech, and we've got to get this right."

We started from the beginning. At last, the moment of the kiss came again. The cold air made my hair stand on end. What was with the cold air? Oh, shoot. The ghost. It was here.

Caleb leaned down and kissed my lips in the most gentle of ways. Despite his tenderness, my blood turned to ice.

As soon as his lips touched mine, a loud popping sound exploded above our heads, and glass rained down. Caleb jumped back, and I sat up abruptly. Glass bit into my hands, and sharp pain stung my palms.

"What the hell?" Jack got up out of his seat.

Miguel yelled, "Close your eyes and don't move!"

What was going on? I did as Miguel said, but I needed to see what was happening.

"Stay put!" Jack's voice was close by. "I don't want you to slip on this."

Bits of glass continued to fall on my head and bounced off my clothes. Finally, it stopped.

"You can open your eyes—and carefully, carefully get off the stage," Miguel said.

Caleb stepped forward and held out his hand to help me to my feet. I didn't take it.

"Are you all right?" he asked.

I was dazed. What just happened? I looked up at the light bar above me. The bulbs had exploded. Jagged glass glinted ominously over our heads.

"Best not to look up," Caleb said. "Glass might still come down and get in your eyes." He took my hand. "You're bleeding."

"I know." I winced and yanked my hands back. I turned my palms up, and inspected them. "I guess I must have gotten a few shards of glass in my skin."

"Miguel, can you get the tweezers out of the first aid kit?" Jack asked.

"Yup, be right back," he answered.

Jack leaned over from below the stage. "Give me your arm, Jenny."

He helped me down and led me over to one of the seats. "Miguel will get the bits of glass out." He ran his fingers through his hair. "In all of my thirty years with this theatre, I have never, ever seen anything like this happen." He took a deep breath and blew it out slowly. "It's almost like this show is cursed."

Cursed. Well, that was a good word for it.

We walked out to the lobby. Everyone had left the theatre while the adults cleaned up the glass. We sat on the red and gold carpet. Nervous whispers filled the room.

The glass doors opened. Two men walked over to the office. The taller guy had a tape measure and a clipboard. The other was wearing a suit jacket and trousers. They spoke to the business manager.

"Who are those guys?" Ross scrutinized the men.

Madeline shrugged. "I have no idea."

Caleb moved over to me. "Are you all right?" he asked, touching my arm.

I scooted away slightly, and bit my lip. "Yeah, I guess so. Are you?" I narrowed my eyes at him. He had been stalking and threatening me for quite some time now.

I tried to read his thoughts, but I detected nothing but concern. There were no violent or hostile vibes coming from him. Weird.

"Is the executive director available?" the man in the suit jacket asked the business manager.

"Let me check." She picked up the phone. "Marcus, can you come down? There are some gentlemen here to see you."

Ross came over and sat down next to me.

"I wonder who those guys are." I pointed at the men. I had a strange feeling about them.

"I think they're the contractors the school district hired." He had a scowl on his face.

"School district?"

"Yeah," Caleb said. "Haven't you heard the news about our building?"

I shrugged. I vaguely remembered something about that. "Maybe a little. What's up?"

"The school district owns this building—but they need to tear it down to build an elementary school."

"What?" I was shocked. Then I remembered the comment from one of the audience members during the Halloween show. Something about the school district tearing down the theatre. I thought it was a joke. This was such a nice theatre and a second home for so many kids. "But what will happen to YTN? Do we have a place to go?"

"Youth Theatre Northwest has been around for thirty years," Caleb said. "I'm sure it will survive."

"I hope so. But it's a shame this building will be torn down." Again, an icy chill raised the hairs on the back of my neck. I shifted my legs underneath me. I wanted to wrap my arms around myself, but my hands were still bloody.

"Are you cold?" Caleb tried putting his arm around me.

I jumped to my feet. "I thought Miguel was supposed to bring the tweezers to get the glass out of my hands. I'll go find him." No way was I going to let that creep put his arm around me.

The double doors to the auditorium opened, and Miguel came out with a first aid kit.

"You read my mind." I stepped forward and held my hands out. It was a relief to get away from stalker dude.

Miguel smiled. "Have a seat, Jenny."

I walked to the opposite wall from where Caleb was, and sat down on the floor.

Miguel took out the tweezers and some antibacterial ointment. After a few seconds, he said, "It's not too bad really. Just a couple of big chunks, but I can get those out in a jiffy."

I winced as he tugged them out of my skin.

The men standing by the office turned to stare at us. "What happened in there?" the guy with the tape measure asked.

Without looking up, Miguel said, "Just a freak accident. One of the lights exploded. Might be faulty wiring."

"Good thing you won't have to worry about that in a few months," the guy wearing the suit said.

Miguel muttered something under his breath.

Marcus, the executive director, came down the hall into the lobby, and approached the men. "Can I help you with something?"

Suit man adjusted his tie. "Can we talk somewhere privately?"

"Yeah, sure." Marcus exchanged a glance with Miguel and motioned for the men to go back down the hall.

I studied Miguel's face. His dark eyebrows were furrowed as he inspected my palms for remaining shards of glass.

"Are they really going to demolish this building?"

He sighed. "Yes." He noted the alarm on my face. "Don't worry, it will be okay. There's a church around the corner that is willing to take us in for the next few years."

"A church? But how can that work for performance space?"

"They have a hall that can hold about the same number of people as our Studio Stage. We'll have to rent bigger stages elsewhere for our big Main Stage shows."

"But why would the school district do this?"

"It's their property. They have a right to take it back— it's not like they're bad people. It's just that the current school situation won't hold the number of kids they have. They need more room. Don't worry, we'll figure it out."

Cold air swooshed past me. Miguel shivered and looked over his shoulder. "Besides, this place is getting weirder and weirder by the minute."

Chapter 23

Tech week. In theatre terms, this meant that we needed to arrive in full make-up, get changed into our costumes immediately, and be ready to warm up on stage at the stroke of six o'clock, or else.

Benny rode with me, since he was working the soundboard for the show.

We stopped at the light on the freeway off-ramp. I whipped out my lipstick and applied it quickly. The light turned green, and I shoved the makeup bag toward Benny. "Here. Put this in my purse, will ya?"

He rolled his eyes. "You girls and your primping."

"I'm not primping. It's a requirement. It's tech week." I gunned it and turned to go up Gallagher Hill.

"Slow down there, Lightning McQueen, the cop shop is right there."

I huffed. "But we can't be late."

"We'll be later if we get a ticket." Benny yawned and stretched. He took out his phone and looked at the time. "Maybe if you go one mile over, you won't get busted. We're about to be late."

I gritted my teeth, and watched the speedometer carefully as we drove up the steep hill.

"You seem really on edge," he said.

"I don't like being late." I squinted through the late afternoon sun and pulled down my visor.

He scrutinized my face. "No, it's more than that. I can tell."

I sighed. "As you know, there's a lot of weird stuff going on at the theatre." I explained the latest developments.

"So, Caleb is coming on to you, yet he's stalking you and calling you a slut and a whore?"

"Yes." I stopped at the four-way at the top of the hill.

"And the ghost is causing earthquakes in the costume closet, and exploding the lights on stage, and trying to kill you with a dagger."

"Uh-huh." I turned right.

"And the building is going to be torn down so the school district can build a new school?"

"Yup." I stopped at the next four-way stop.

"Damn!" Benny's eyes were practically bulging out of his head. "That's messed up."

"I know." I turned left into the YTN parking lot.

Benny grabbed my arm as we pulled into a spot. "Wait a minute."

"What?" I pulled the key out of the ignition.

"Something's not right."

I crossed my arms. "None of this is right. Geesh."

"No, I mean. Caleb can't be the one stalking you—and he doesn't like you the way you think he likes you."

"What do you mean?"

"I mean, I'm not sure Caleb rolls that way—if you know what I mean."

I scrunched up my face. "Huh?"

"That time I met him at your house? Back when the cast was first bonding, and we watched a movie?"

"Yeah…"

"I shook his hand. And—well, I got the distinct feeling he was attracted to you a little. But he was also attracted to me."

"What?"

"Think about it, Jenny. I think Caleb is bisexual. You even mentioned it to me when you first started rehearsals. Remember?"

I massaged my temples. "Yeah, but then the weird texting and stalking started up. So, I figured—"

Benny frowned. "You figured wrong. Last night, I had a vision of him asking me out." His frown transformed into a dreamy gaze. "He's kind of cute, don't you think?"

"Oh, brother." I opened my car door. "Dude, we're a minute late. Besides, I'm worried you might be falling for a crazy person."

Benny got out, slammed the door, and ran for the lobby. "I'm telling you," he puffed over his shoulder as he ran, "he's not crazy. He's cute."

I shook my head and chased after him. I sure hoped his intuition was right. But if it was, who was my stalker?

***

"Let's take a ten minute break, guys," Jack said. "We need to reset the lights."

Good. I needed to talk to Caleb. I had to find out for sure if he was my stalker or not. I wasn't going to confront him—I just wanted to test the waters to see if I could pick up any hints.

If Benny was right, and Caleb was attracted to *him*, and not me, then I was going to have to call Celine. I was sure she could help me figure out who was sending me all those disturbing text messages.

In the lobby, I scanned through the actors, but didn't see him.

Ross was standing over by the bench. I slid in between people and sidled up next to him. "Have you seen Caleb?" I asked.

"I think he went to the bathroom, but I'm not sure."

My phone buzzed in my pocket. I shivered. I took it out and glanced at the screen.

"Whore," it read.

"What the…" Anger and fear hit me all at once. I whirled around, expecting to see someone—anyone with their phone out.

The boys' bathroom door swung open, and Caleb walked out. It had to be him. Who else could it be?

I marched over and poked him in the chest. "Let me see your phone." My body tensed.

Caleb took a step back. "What?"

"Your phone. Hand it over."

"Why should I give you my phone?" His hand rubbed the back of his neck. The kid was a really good actor.

A couple of the other students turned to stare at us. Let them. I was going to put a stop to this once and for all.

Benny appeared at my side, and tried to pull me back. "Jenny—"

I widened my stance. "No, I really need to see his phone."

Caleb frowned and looked back and forth from Benny to me.

"Oh, come on. You can't be serious. I know you've been sending me those texts." I gave him a glare and put my hand out.

"Texts?"

"Don't play dumb, Caleb. The texts that call me a slut and a whore. The texts that tell me to stay away from other boys?"

"What are you talking about?" Color tinted his cheeks.

I put my hands on my hips.

Caleb shook his head and took his phone out of his pocket.

I snatched it away and began scrolling through his texts. Nothing.

Shoot. Did I just go off on this guy for nothing? I felt a lump in my throat, and heat crept from my neck to my face.

Benny gave me a sideways glance. He clapped his hands. "That was awesome, Jenny! Way to go."

What was he doing?

"Yeah, that was great." He patted me on the back.

Caleb looked at us like we were both nuts.

"You see, our drama coach at Newport challenged us to create a scene in our real lives. The assignment was to make the scene so believable, that no one would know it wasn't real. I think Jen here did a bang up job, don't you?" Benny grinned.

A couple of actors standing behind Caleb cracked up.

He still appeared frazzled. "Oh. Yeah, that was really good. You got me."

I barked out a nervous laugh. "I got you, all right! You bought it hook, line, and sinker. Would you give that an A+, Benny?" I leaned in and nudged him. "Thank you," I whispered in his ear.

"Caleb, what's your favorite acting exercise?" Benny took Caleb's arm and led him away from me. Their conversation faded as they left me standing behind.

Benny had saved me from making a huge ass of myself. I made a mental note to treat him to a Starbucks.

Now I was more confused than ever. Caleb was definitely not my stalker. So, who was?

***

"Celine?" I closed the door to my bedroom and breathlessly vaulted onto my bed.

"Jenny, is that you?" Her voice sounded tinny through the cell phone.

"I need your help." I explained everything that had been going on with both the ghost and the stalker.

"My goodness. That's a very complicated problem," she said. "A while ago, I asked you to try talking to the ghost? Have you done that?"

I hesitated. "He seems intent on killing me. I don't know if I can get a word in edgewise."

"Then you must proceed with caution. Talk to him. If his anger flares, you need to be ready to get out. But if he does respond to you, tell him he isn't alive anymore. He needs to move on to the other side."

"I'll do my best. But what about my stalker? Who is he? It's obviously not Caleb."

I could hear Celine breathing deeply on the other end. She was trying to tune into the energy. Finally, she let out a long puff of breath. "It's strange. I'm not getting anything."

"Shoot."

"Yeah, it's odd," she said. "It's as if there is a black wall blocking me from the information. I can't get past it."

I made a disgruntled noise. "This is driving me nuts! Everything is messed up, and I'll never figure things out."

"You're rushing it," Celine said decidedly. "You need to pull back. Breathe. Focus on the problem. Meditate. Pray. Ask for divine guidance."

She was right. I was practically manic—rushing from one conclusion to another. I had to stop being so frantic. What did I do when I needed to find Callie? I used a candle and asked for help. The answers hadn't come right away, but I did get a few clues that steered me in the right direction. I bit my lip. In Alaska, I had been able to project myself into an animal's body—to see through its eyes. Could I do that to find out more clues as to who my stalker was? And maybe I could check up on that ghost too.

I told Celine my thoughts.

"Good. Use what you've learned about your gift to help you through this. You need stillness and an open mind to discover the answers."

"Thank you, Celine. I think I know what to do."

"Keep me posted." She hung up.

Chapter 24

I had so many threads to follow: the stalker and the ghost... and I had nearly forgotten that Ty and Cassandra were coming to town in just a couple of days. The reminder of their impending visit sent waves of panic through me—we would be visiting the UW. That meant there was a possibility of us running into Mike. Mike and Ty face-to-face. How would I handle that?

I groaned and crawled under the covers of my bed. One thing at a time, I reminded myself. I pulled the blankets up to my chin. Honestly, if I could just be an ostrich and hide my head in the sand, that would be fine with me. I was of the firm belief that not dealing with any of it seemed like the best option. But then I thought of the scary texts I'd been getting. And the angry ghost. Ignoring those issues could get me killed.

Projecting myself into some sort of animal to spy on the ghost seemed like the path of least resistance. I could remove myself from the animal if things got scary. Then I would be back in my bed, safe and warm.

But what sort of animal could I inhabit? The ghost was inside a dark theatre. The only kind of animal I had ever seen in the theatre was... ugh. A rat. I shuddered. It seemed as though nothing about this situation was going to be easy. From the time I was a little girl, I had been terrified of rats. Those beady little eyes, yellowed teeth and that long, naked tail... My stomach lurched. I resisted the urge to throw up. It had to be done.

I closed my eyes and conjured up the memory of the rat I had seen skittering down the hall of YTN several weeks before. Madeline and I had shrieked and run to the lobby—the boys mocking us as we fled. I was sure it was the same rat I saw on Halloween night in the narrow staircase going up to the costume shop. That rat was probably still alive, lurking in the empty, black space.

I took a deep breath and let it out slowly. I imagined the rat. Gray body. Black eyes. Twitching nose. What was it doing at this very moment? I let myself fall into a light trance, and tried to think rat-like thoughts.

Suddenly, I was in the auditorium. It was pitch-black, except for the glowing green exit lights hanging above the doors. I let my eyes adjust to the dark. I sat up on my haunches and sniffed the air. Just the lingering scent of smelly feet and old gum stuck to the bottom of the seats.

Nosing my way through the rows of seats, I arrived at the end where the stairs angled up to the stage. I sniffed again. I was just about to climb the stairs, when a smoky haze materialized in the center of the stage. I froze, not daring to move.

Was it him? I scurried up the stairs and hid under the edge of the heavy curtain. My tail twitched, and then froze when I realized it might capture his attention.

I watched as the haze turned into a solid figure of a young man. A solitary light popped on overhead—casting a spotlight directly over him.

He had blond hair and was of average height. He was the ghost from Halloween night, But where else had I seen him? He looked vaguely familiar. My whiskers twitched. I had seen him in my dreams. The boy who seemed rough and menacing with his girlfriend—with me.

The boy turned his body out to the audience. In a loud voice, he said,

"Arms, take your last embrace! and, lips, O you
The doors of breath, seal with a righteous kiss
A dateless bargain to engrossing death!
Come, bitter conduct, come, unsavoury guide!
Thou desperate pilot, now at once run on
The dashing rocks thy sea-sick weary bark!
Here's to my love!"

He took a sip from a bottle that suddenly appeared in his hand.

"O true apothecary!
Thy drugs are quick. Thus with a kiss I die."

The light shone down on his face, making the hollows of his cheeks exaggerated. He looked out at the audience again. Was he expecting a response? But the seats were dark. His body contorted, as if the poison had hit its mark deep within. He crumpled to the stage, lying prone on the wood.

His eyes closed for a moment, and then opened.

I fidgeted under the curtain. My whiskers were rubbing on the sides of the fabric, making my nose itch.

He turned his face to me. I held my breath, suppressing the urge to twitch.

Anger turned his eyes to slits. "You were supposed to die. I told you. It was you and me together until the end!" he raged. His fist pounded the floor.

Holy crap! Who did he think I was? I was just a little rat. Did he have some sort of rodent vendetta? I shrunk back into the folds of the heavy velvet.

A dagger appeared in his hand. His body became hazy once again. The mist retained the angry face while the rest of his body blurred.

His ghostly hands grabbed the curtain and shook it. I darted out from under the heavy fabric and ran to the center of the stage.

"Argh!" He shifted around and glided toward me menacingly. "I see you, my dear Juliet. You can't get away."

I squeaked and ran toward the wings. Boxes and props were stored haphazardly in a jumble. A crate, turned upside down, was pushed far off into the corner. I squeezed myself through the bottom crack, and crouched down, making myself as small as possible.

He thought I was Juliet? But couldn't he see I was a rat?

"I know who you are. Did you think you could fool me?" he growled.

It sounded like he was only inches away. I hitched in a breath. I really needed to get out of this animal and escape to safety.

With a whoop of triumph, he flipped the crate over, exposing me to his rage.

Like a deer caught in headlights, my brain seized up. I couldn't move. His misty body solidified before me, knife in hand.

I let out a piercing screech. My brain unfroze and I rushed forward, between his feet. I zigzagged back and forth as he swiped at me with the dagger.

"Three blind mice," he said in a really creepy, sing-song way.

My little heart was thrashing in my chest. I ran forward and then snapped backward as he stepped on the end of my long tail. My claws scrabbled against the wood floor. Frantically, I tried to pull myself out of the rat body. But my thoughts were so distressed, I couldn't concentrate enough to get out.

His body changed once again to the silver mist. It remained just solid enough to retain his facial features, now twisted with hatred. He swooped to my level—his eyes huge before me. His daggered hand struck out at me. "DIE!"

Terror gripped me, but also allowed me one moment where my thoughts were not spiraling out of control. I ripped myself out of the rat's body, swirling into confused darkness.

Relief washed over me. I felt the softness of my own bed beneath me. I felt my cheeks, the smooth skin reaffirming that I was in my own body. I shivered.

That was too close for comfort. That—thing—was diabolical. Reasoning with him had been a pipe dream. No, I would have to approach this another way. And I would need help.

Chapter 25

I flipped over onto my side. No matter how hard I tried, I couldn't fall asleep. I kept replaying the rat scene over and over. The ghost had said that he knew who I was. Did he? He called me his Juliet. Clearly, I was not Juliet—and he was no Romeo.

A thought struck me from out of the blue.

He called me Juliet. He was reciting a soliloquy from *Romeo and Juliet*. So—he thought of himself as Romeo. Or, he *played* Romeo. And so his Juliet…

That was it! I sat bolt upright in bed. This guy was stuck there. Something happened between himself and the girl who played Juliet. But what?

I got up and pushed the power button on my laptop. It was an older model, so it took a while to load. While I waited, I paced, wearing a path on the carpet between my bed and my desk. What would make a ghost so angry? Usually that kind of anger was caused by heightened emotion. Loss? Betrayal? Betrayal felt right to me. The girl who played Juliet had betrayed the boy who had played Romeo. What had he said again? My mind flicked back to the stage, where I watched him as he crumpled to the wooden floor.

He'd said, *"You were supposed to die. I told you. It was you and me together until the end!"*

You and me together… until the end. The end.

The computer screen glowed; the login screen blinked at me.

I sat down in my chair and loaded the browser. What kind of query would get me the results I needed. I typed in "*Romeo and Juliet* incident Youth Theatre Northwest." I pressed enter and waited.

A bunch of random stuff about *Romeo and Juliet* surfaced. Most of the returns had nothing to do with YTN. I clicked through the first few pages of results. Nothing.

A dozen other searches delivered nothing. I must not have come up with the right search terms. What I really needed was… another dream. My visions often came in dreams. But I had been so caught up with the school, rehearsals, and the stress of the stalker, I had neglected to sleep a good, deep sleep.

I did feel a little sleepy now. I closed my laptop and crawled back into bed. I closed my eyes and breathed deeply. "Please send me a dream to help me find out more about the ghost," I said softly to the universe or anyone who might be listening. "I need more information about the boy who played Romeo."

I curled up, hugging my pillow and fell asleep.

It was dark except for the disco ball twirling over the dance floor. Livin' on a Prayer blasted out from the speakers anchoring the corners of the stage. The DJ, wearing dark sunglasses, sifted through a rack of albums.

Suddenly, I was aware of myself in this space. And holy hell, I was much more aware in this dream than I had ever been in any other dream or vision.

The colors were real. The people seemed real.

I sat at a table with a few girls. I stared down at my dress. I looked like freakin' Madonna. Strapless, black. With a poofy tulle skirt. I even had a black lace glove on my left hand. I grimaced. The 80s.

I scanned through the people dancing or standing around. Looking for him.

There he was, in a group of about eight or nine guys. He looked haughty—they hung on his every word. Blond, average height, good-looking.

"Do you want to dance?" A boy stepped into view from the shadows.

He was kind of short, but well-muscled, and handsome.

My eyes flicked to the girls sitting with me. Their eyes darted nervously to the blond boy joking with his cronies.

"Uh, sure?" Not knowing if I had said the right thing, I hesitantly got up from my chair and moved to the dance floor with the dark-haired boy.

The song changed to a ballad. Crap. Slow dance.

The boy put his hands awkwardly on my waist. I took a breath. My hands rested on his shoulders.

We stepped back and forth, not quite in rhythm. The chatter around us quieted. I looked at the sea of faces around us—and they were all staring.

Heart beating loudly in my chest, I looked for the blond boy. Romeo.

And there he was, arms crossed, his face turning a darker shade of red every few seconds.

Uh oh.

I glanced nervously at the dark-haired boy I was dancing with. He was clueless.

I released his shoulders and backed away.

He looked confused. "Something wrong?"

I tipped my head toward Romeo. "I think so."

The dark-haired boy's eyes caught sight him. "Oh—I didn't know…"

Romeo charged.

He grabbed me by the arm, digging his fingers into my flesh.

"Hey!" the dark-haired guy yelled. "Leave her alone."

Romeo whirled around and smacked his fist into the other guy's nose. A sickening crunch registered loudly over the din of the music. His hands flew to his face, blood cascading down in a rush and pooling onto his white shirt.

I turned and ran into the crowd, searching for the exit. Romeo chased after me. "Come back here!"

I almost made it to the door. But a cold, hard grip on my shoulder yanked me back. I turned to face him. His face was a mask of anger.

"I told you," he said quietly. The danger in his voice cut the air like a blade. "You are mine. Forever."

I tried to struggle free from his grip.

"Mine!" His arm swung back and then whipped forward as he struck me hard.

"Jenny! Are you all right?" Mom was shaking me gently. "You woke up the whole household with your screams."

I gulped in air and tried to sit up. "He hit me."

"Who hit you?" Mom gave me a worried look.

"Romeo."

Her brows furrowed. "Romeo?"

I sighed. "There is something I need to tell you."

The door burst open. It was Jackson. His eyes were red-rimmed. "Mom! I had a dream. A really, really bad dream."

Mom looked back and forth from me to Jackson. "Did it involve a guy named Romeo?"

Jackson was awestruck. "Yeah—how did you know?" He crossed the room in seconds and flung himself onto the bed next to Mom.

He whimpered and she wrapped her arms around him. "What did you see?"

Jackson pulled himself together a little, and took a breath. "This guy. His name was Romeo. He was on this stage somewhere, I don't know. And this girl—she was wearing a long green dress. It looked like a costume maybe."

"Go on." Mom wiped the tears from his face.

"And then he said, 'We're doing this together, right?' He handed her a bottle of pills—and he had a bottle for himself."

I swallowed hard. "Then what happened?" I asked, even though I already knew.

Jackson's face blanched. "She didn't look too sure about it. I could tell she was scared. But he said, 'On the count of three. He counted, and they both opened their bottles. Romeo poured all of the pills in his mouth—I mean all of them. And he swallowed them all down with his bottle of water."

I leaned in. "What did the girl do, Jackson?"

"She tried to swallow them. But she was scared, and she kept gagging and spitting them back out. The guy—he flipped out when she didn't get the pills down. He grabbed her and pushed her down on the stage. He was angry. He screamed in her face, and shook her."

"Oh, God." Mom paled too, and her voice trembled.

"Then he sat on her, and he tried opening her mouth and forcing her to swallow the pills. But the girl screamed and screamed. I think she might've bitten him. He hit her and hit her until her face was swollen and bleeding."

A shiver ran down my spine. That poor girl. His Juliet.

Jackson took in a hiccupping gasp of air. "Finally, the guy slowed down. He couldn't hit hard anymore—and he slumped over on top of the girl." He looked down at his hands. "He was dead."

I got up and moved to the other side of Jackson and put my arm around him. "I'm so sorry, little brother."

He looked up at me, his face ashen. "Is this the kind of stuff that you see all the time?"

I nodded grimly. "I know it's scary, buddy, but you get used to it after a while. And if you learn to use your gift, you can actually help people."

Jackson's eyes blurred with tears. "But I don't want it. I don't like seeing things like this."

I pulled him in close and hugged him like I'd never hugged him before. "I'll help you. It's going to be okay."

***

In the kitchen, the kettle whistled. Mom turned off the burner and poured hot water into three large mugs.

"Can I have whipped cream on my cocoa?" Jackson sniffled.

"Of course, honey." Mom joined us at the table and set down our mugs with spoons, a can of whipped cream, and a bag of mini-marshmallows. "Knock yourselves out."

I took a tiny sip of mine. It was too hot. I cupped my hands around the warm mug and tried to think comforting thoughts.

We stared gloomily into our hot chocolate—no one speaking a word.

Finally, Mom cleared her throat. "Obviously, there is something to these dreams you are both having." She turned to me, "I believe you know more about this than either Jackson or myself. Care to fill us in?"

I sighed and took a sip of my cocoa, feeling the warmth trickle down my throat. "It's late. Are you sure you want to hear it now?"

She gave me a stern look, and crossed her arms.

"Okay, but it might take a while." I told Mom and Jackson everything—well, almost everything. I hadn't decided whether or not to talk about the stalker. I was afraid if my parents knew, they wouldn't ever let me leave the house.

"This Romeo ghost sounds dangerous to me," she said. "We can't let this go on indefinitely. We're going to need some help."

"You mean, like help from Celine?"

"Maybe. But you also have other psychic friends as well, don't you? What about that older man, Frank? Or Benny?" she asked.

"Frank is busy with his family. I don't want to bother him. Benny, on the other hand, can definitely help."

"It might be wise to get Celine too. I'd feel better knowing there was an adult with, uh, experience with this sort of thing. Do you think she'll come?"

"She hasn't been much help. I've already talked to her a couple of times about this ghost. She just keeps telling me to talk to him. I don't think she understands how scary he is."

"Maybe if you make her understand…"

"I'll call her." I looked at the clock. It was three o'clock in the morning. "Later."

We finished our hot cocoa and put the dishes in the sink.

"Let's try to get some sleep." Mom gently pushed us out of the kitchen.

"*Try* being the operative word," I muttered. In addition to being shaken by what we'd just learned about the ghost, I was also kind of glad. The pieces were starting to come together. Maybe we could find a resolution to this craziness after all.

Chapter 26

Today was the day that Ty and Cassandra were flying in from Sitka. And after last night's family ghost dreams, my nerves were on edge. Double the nerves, double the fun.

My locker door banged shut, and my hands shook as I slung my backpack onto my shoulder. What was I so on edge about? These were good friends. Nothing to worry about. But then I thought of Mike and I shuddered. Did I still have feelings for Ty? Would he still have feelings for me?

"Hey!" Benny jogged to catch up to me. "Okay if I tag along with you to the airport?"

"I'm not leaving without you." I grabbed his arm and squeezed it.

Benny stopped walking. "You're nervous, aren't you?"

I looked down at my feet.

"Is it because of the Mike and Ty thing?" He took one look at my face and patted my shoulder.

I let out a long breath and felt my face growing redder by the minute.

"You're dating Mike again, so isn't it settled? Ty knows you're dating Mike."

I made a face.

"Doesn't he?"

I started walking faster toward the exit.

"Wait!" Benny ran after me. "You didn't *tell* him?"

"It never came up." I pushed the double doors open.

Benny rushed past me and then whirled around and blocked me from going any further. "It never came up?" He gave me a skeptical look.

I pushed a strand of hair out of my face. "No, it didn't. Ty has barely talked to me since I came back to Seattle. He was grieving. The poor guy didn't need to deal with relationship stuff, and I was fine with that."

"So, you didn't tell him."

"Right. And besides, Mike and I are dating, but it's not that serious." I bit my lip. "Honestly, I don't feel tied to either guy right now. I mean, I care about both of them—but things are different."

Benny gave me a wry look. "Seriously, Jenny? I think the problem is that you have feelings for both guys. You just can't decide which one you like more."

Damn that kid. He always knew what I was thinking or feeling. I closed my eyes and took a deep breath. "Benny…"

"I know, I know. I'm always right—and that can be irritating, but you're going to have to figure this out sooner rather than later. What time does their flight arrive?"

"Three o'clock." I glanced at the time on my cell phone screen. "We' better leave now to beat rush-hour traffic."

***

"I can't believe how many people are at the airport." Benny peered ahead at the mass of taxis, cars, and shuttles all vying for a position for the curb in the Arrivals section.

The Alaska Airlines curb was not too far ahead, but the sheer number of vehicles trying to merge in and out was ridiculous. We crawled forward at a snail's pace.

Finally, I scooted my car up next to the pick-up area.

Benny jumped out of the car and craned his neck, trying to see through the airport's tall windows.

My heart pounded in my chest. Would Ty try to kiss me? Maybe he was completely over me. Maybe not. I wiped my palms on my jeans.

"There they are!" Benny shouted, startling me.

I opened the car door and joined him on the sidewalk. The glass doors slid open, and a wall of sound greeted me.

"OMG! Jenny!" Cassandra rushed toward me, the wheels of her large suitcase wobbling dangerously as she yanked it along.

I was hit full force by a spatter of freckles and curly auburn hair. She squeezed me so tightly, I couldn't breathe.

I grinned, unable to contain my joy at seeing my bubbly friend.

The top of her head barely cleared my chin. She was chattering about the flight, and the lack of good snack material on the plane—and still, she held on to me tightly. "Can you believe there were only six peanuts in the entire bag?"

She pulled back from me and held me at arms' length. "Six! What do I look like, a hamster? I mean six peanuts! What would happen if the plane crashed on some remote island? I'd be dead by the next day from lack of nourishment." She clicked her tongue and shook her head. "Whatever happened to the good old days, when they actually fed you a sandwich? I mean sure, they weren't all that tasty, but at least it was filling."

I patted her shoulder. "We'll stop and get you some food, okay?"

Cassandra spotted Benny. "OMG! My gay, psychic friend!"

While Benny was being mauled, I glanced at the door. Ty stood just outside it, watching the incident unfold with a fond grin on his face. His gaze shifted to me, and he broke into a smile that lit the whole world, dimples and all.

My heart, which had been strained with the anxiety of seeing Ty again, ached with a new desire to hold him.

145

Before I had time to feel guilty about Mike, Ty crossed the space between us and pulled me into a tight hug. His scent was intoxicating—a mixture of the deep, spicy aroma of cedar and the wildly free fragrance of the ocean. My heart pounded against my ribs.

We hugged and laughed, swaying back and forth as if some internal tune played only for us.

Finally, I pulled away, only to see Benny and Cassandra staring at us with their mouths hanging open. I gulped and felt color blooming into my cheeks. What was I doing?

Benny mouthed, "Sparks!"

Cassandra furrowed her brows. She knew about Mike. During the summer, I had told her he had broken up with me. Later, I had texted her that we were dating again. Not being able to hide anything from anybody, Cassandra's thoughts were written all over her face. It was almost as if she'd said out loud, "What? Oh! Really? You still like him. But what about your boyfriend?"

Before she could verbalize, I wiped my own emotions off my face, stepped away from Ty, and grabbed Cassandra's luggage to put in the trunk of my car.

Her head whipped back and forth from me to Ty to Benny, and back to me again.

"Here, Cassandra, why don't you and Ty have a seat in the back?" I opened the door for them.

Ty looked confused, but got in and buckled his seat belt.

I slid into the driver's seat, avoiding eye contact with Benny. My knuckles were white on the steering wheel. I took a breath and forced lightness into my voice. "So, Cassandra—I know you're hungry. What kind of food would you like? Mexican, Italian, Indian?"

At the mention of food, Cassandra perked up. "Any restaurant that serves burgers and bacon. Bacon burgers!"

I laughed. "I'd almost forgotten how much you love bacon."

"If you were just going for the burger part, I would suggest Dick's Drive-In. That's the classic Seattle burger joint," Benny offered. "But I don't think they serve bacon burgers there."

"No," Cassandra whispered, disappointment clouding her eyes.

"They don't." I looked over my shoulder and pulled away from the curb. "But Burgermaster has a killer bacon burger…with cheese."

Cassandra bounced in her seat. "Yes! Bacon and cheese. A winning combination." Her smile filled my rear-view mirror.

I caught a glimpse of Ty rolling his eyes next to her.

"University District or Bellevue location?" I asked Benny.

"U-District."

Just then, a thought occurred to me. "Ty! What about your mom? I thought she was coming with you."

He leaned forward. "My grandfather has a touch of pneumonia, so Mom decided to stay home and keep an eye on him."

"Is he okay?" I worried about Henry. Ty's grandfather was a wise man, a shaman. But he was definitely getting up there in years.

"He'll be fine. It's walking pneumonia—not the kind that puts you in the hospital."

Cassandra's face screwed up and her lips pooched out. "Walking pneumonia. It sounds like a zombie thing. You know—like that TV show?"

I snorted. "That's *The Walking Dead*. And the virus they've got isn't pneumonia. I'll guarantee that."

Benny shook his head. "Let's also remember that zombies aren't real."

Cassandra shrugged. "Well, I hope Henry will be okay."

***

The crowd at Burgermaster was just thinning out. We found a table for the four of us in the corner and sat down with our trays of burgers, fries, and milkshakes.

Cassandra's eyes glazed over as she took her first bite of her bacon cheeseburger. "Ohmigod." She grabbed a handful of fries and stuffed them into her mouth, her cheeks bulging like a chipmunk preparing for winter.

Ty sat across from me, looking both amused and disgusted with Cassandra's lack of table manners. His phone bleeped and he glanced at the screen. "Oh, no."

"What?" Cassandra said in between bites. A fry fell out of her mouth and landed on her lap. She picked it up and popped it back in, chewing vigorously.

"Do they not feed you at home?" I asked.

"Oh, they do!" She nodded enthusiastically. "But I thought I told you, I'm not allowed to eat junk food. And this right here," she waved her hand at the bounty in front of her, "is exactly what my parents would be very much against."

Benny pointed at Ty's phone. "Anything wrong?"

Ty scrolled through his messages. "Actually, yeah. My mom said the hotel double-booked our rooms. They gave them away to someone else and there aren't any other rooms available. There's a convention or something going on."

Cassandra swallowed and she put her mostly-eaten burger down on her tray. "You mean, we have no place to stay?"

"I guess not." Ty paled.

Cassandra's eyes welled up with tears. "But I don't want to sleep on park benches."

An idea struck me. "You could stay at my house."

148

"Really?" Her lips quivered. "You would do that?"

"Sure. Let me check with Mom." I whipped out my cell and texted her.

Her reply came within seconds. "Of course. What time?"

"We'll be there in an hour," I texted back.

I grinned. "She said yes."

Cassandra jumped out of her chair and let out a whoop. "Awesome!"

Customers turned their heads to stare at her, and she sat down abruptly. Ty gave me a flirtatious smile, and a blush crept up his cheeks.

The door opened, and I tore my eyes away from Ty's face. In walked Mike and two pretty college girls, both with long, straight blond hair—like mine.

My stunned look caught the attention of my friends, who followed my gaze.

"I don't blame you for staring, Jenny. That guy is super hot." Cassandra winked at me.

Benny looked mortified. "Holy hell."

Ty's gaze flicked from Mike to Benny and me. "What... what's going on?"

Just then, Mike caught sight of me. Surprise lit his face and he broke into a wide grin. He said something to his companions and headed my way.

Panic rose in my chest. It was too soon. I hadn't told Ty about Mike yet. I wasn't prepared to deal with this.

"Jenny!"

I rose from my chair, numb from the shock.

Mike scooped me into a bone crushing hug. "Babe! You didn't tell me you would be in the U-District today."

He bent down and kissed me fully on the lips.

Ty blanched.

My face burned.

The buzz from my pocket split the horrifying silence.

"Filthy whore," the text read.

149

***

Between the horror of my worst nightmare coming true with Mike meeting Ty and the jarring text from my stalker, I felt like I was going to pass out. I took one more glance at my phone and then shoved it into my pocket. My eyes roamed around the restaurant, hoping to catch a glimpse of anyone that looked suspicious. My gaze shifted back to Ty and then to Mike.

Mike stepped back and looked at my friends sitting at the table. He noticed Ty's expression and the astounded looks on Cassandra and Benny's faces. "Aren't you going to introduce me to your friends?" He smiled uncertainly at me.

"Uh, yeah." I wiped my sweaty hands on my jeans. "Mike, these are my friends, Benny, Cassandra, and Ty."

"Ty," Mike repeated.

I could almost see the wheels turning in his head. I had told Mike about Ty on one of our recent dates.

"Well, it's nice to meet you all." Mike looked a little shaken.

"Aren't you going to introduce me to *your* friends?" I motioned toward the two blondes who had migrated closer to our table.

"God, I'm sorry." His face reddened. "This is Sarah, and Nicole."

The girls smiled and said hello.

Mike backed away from the table. "Well, I don't want to take any more of your time. We're just picking up some food to go."

Oh my God. I screwed this up so badly. "Before you order, can I talk to you outside?"

"Uh, okay." He turned to his friends. "Can you order for me? I want a bacon burger with cheese."

Cassandra beamed approvingly at him.

150

I grabbed Mike's arm and led him out the door. I could feel the eyes of my friends boring holes into our backs.

***

"Ty, huh?" Mike ran his fingers through this hair. "Why didn't you tell me he was coming here?"

"I'm sorry. I was so busy with school and rehearsals that it completely slipped my mind." I shifted uncomfortably.

I could see the steam rising off him.

"Hey, I wasn't intentionally keeping this from you," I said. "Cassandra's here too. They're going on a college visit."

He grunted. "Is that all, or do you have something else to tell me?"

I went back and forth between being insulted that he didn't trust me and feeling guilty for not telling him that Ty was coming to visit.

"Look, they're truly here on a college visit. Ty ended things with me right before I left Sitka. But he's still a friend, and I do care about him."

Mike stared at his feet.

"Hey." I gently touched his cheek. "We just started dating again. Let's not mess this up before it even begins."

He shifted his attention to my face, his green eyes looking troubled. "And you're sure you don't still want to be with him?"

My stomach clenched in knots. To deny my attraction to Ty would be an outright lie. However, my feelings for the both of them were muddled, and I wasn't thinking clearly. "I still care about Ty." I swallowed hard.

His face couldn't hide his disappointment.

"Look, you broke my heart this summer." I bit my lip. "Literally—it felt like someone had ripped it out of my chest and twisted it until it was dry."

151

Now it was Mike's turn to feel a little guilt; I could read it in his expression.

"Ty came along after I was beginning to heal. My feelings for him were unexpected and uncomplicated. After we found his cousin dead and his aunt barely hanging onto life, he broke things off with me. But I understood. His mom and aunt needed him more than I did. It wasn't hard for me to let him go because of that."

Mike looked like he wanted to interject, but I cut him off before he could say a word.

"You on the other hand, hurt me deeply. So, I'm not ready to fully commit to you. That's why I told you that we needed to start this—whatever *this* is—slowly. If that means that you have to wait for me to sort out my feelings, then you wait. And if you don't want to wait, and you force me to commit to you before I'm ready, then you had better go back to those two Jenny look-alikes. Because I'm not getting my heart broken by you again."

Mike shook his head, and muttered under his breath. "That's not fair. And by the way, those girls are just friends who I met in my dorm. Friends—that's all." He paced in front of me.

"How many times do I have to say I'm sorry?"

"Excuse me?" I put my hand on my hip.

"I said, how many times do I have to apologize for this summer? I screwed up! In a big way. I get it. Don't throw it in my face." He ran his fingers through his hair again. "I feel *terrible* for the pain I caused you. I'm asking you, please. Can you just give us a chance?"

"I'm sorry for bringing it up. But I don't want to lie and say that I don't care about Ty. He's a good friend, and we have a lot in common. I'm not going to stop talking to him or being a friend to him because you're jealous. And I don't expect you to drop those two girls as friends."

The tension went out of his shoulders and the corner of his mouth drew up. "Wait. Are you jealous of Sarah and Nicole?"

I smiled and put my hands in my pockets. "Maybe a tiny bit."

He relaxed and pulled me into a side hug. "Okay, I guess we're kind of even. Sort of." He eyed Ty through the window.

Ty, Cassandra, and Benny were pretending not to look at us.

"Let's go back in." I nudged him toward the door.

"I'll just get my food and head out. The girls are waiting for me at the other entrance," he said.

"Are you going to come for opening night on Friday?" I glanced at my group of friends. "They'll be there too. I hope you're okay with that."

Mike worked hard to smile. "Maybe."

Chapter 27

On the way to my house, there was silence. Not even Cassandra made a peep. Several times I heard her intake of air, as if she were getting ready to say something, but then she quickly blew it out and stared out the window.

I pulled into our driveway and helped to unload the luggage.

"Home, sweet home!" I tried to sound cheerful as I opened the front door. What was Ty thinking? Had the others filled him in about Mike? I felt so bad. I should've told Ty about him. But Ty had only texted with me briefly after this summer's events, and it would've been awkward to bring up my ex-boyfriend turned current boyfriend. Still, the image of his face when Mike kissed me right in front of him—that was etched into my mind and burning a hole there.

Mom greeted us at the door, beaming. "Hello, Sitkans!"

I put on a happy face and led them in. The smell of garlic bread and marinara sauce drifted through the house.

"Smells awesome in here." Cassandra licked her lips.

"Thank you." Mom took the two Alaskans by the arm and showed them upstairs. "Cassandra, you can sleep in Jenny's room. Ty, you'll be in the guest room." Her voice faded as they disappeared down the hall.

Benny nudged me. "That was awkward. What are the odds of having Mike show up the day Ty arrived? Did you do something to the Universe to make it mad at you?"

I shrugged. "I feel too shell-shocked to answer that."

"As much as I love drama," Benny added. "I'm not so crazy about this particular kind."

I eyed him. "Did Ty say anything while I was talking to Mike outside of Burgermaster?"

He shook his head. "Not a word. I mean, I don't think he could even speak."

I let out a heavy sigh. "God. Just shoot me now."

***

Dinner was pleasant, but the unsettled vibe of today's earlier events still lingered in the air. Cassandra, God love her, chattered non-stop about bacon, Sitka, the U-Dub and just about every other thing that crossed her mind.

"And to think," she said, "we could all be going to the University of Washington together! Wouldn't that be fun?"

Not if Mike and Ty would be there together. No, that would not be *fun*. I took a big gulp of my water. It went down the wrong pipe, and I coughed violently. Cassandra pounded my back.

"Ow!" I coughed some more. "I'm fine. Really." I coughed again.

"Did you get spaghetti up your nose?" She peered at my nostrils. "I hate it when that happens."

Benny hid his smile behind his napkin. "Oh, dear lord," he said under his breath.

Ty hadn't spoken much since Burgermaster, but even he couldn't help but laugh a little. At least my almost dying helped to break the ice.

Mom came in from the kitchen. "I heard a strange noise. Is everything all right?"

155

"Did you know about your daughter's drinking problem?" Benny gave Mom a concerned look.

I punched his arm. "That's a tired old joke. I give it a zero for originality."

The others laughed and Mom looked confused. "Guess you had to be there, huh?" She wiped her hands on a towel and turned to go back into the kitchen.

That did it. We burst into a fit of laughter—relieved that the heavy blanket of awkwardness had been lifted.

***

I was in my PJs and thinking about the next day. Tomorrow was our U-Dub visit. The thought of having another run-in with Mike made my stomach hurt. I still hadn't spoken to Ty about Mike, and I figured if I was going to get any sleep at all, I would need to go talk to him. Cassandra was already snoring on the air mattress we set up in my room. Her blanket was pulled up to her chin, and she was muttering something in her sleep. I almost laughed out loud—she never stopped talking, not even during R.E.M.

I snuck out of my room and tiptoed down the hall to the guest room. My heart pounded in my chest. My hand hovered up to the door. Would he be asleep already? Maybe it would be better if I talked to him later. I let my hand fall to my side. No. He deserved to know.

Before I lost my courage again, I lifted my hand back up and knocked softly.

"Yes?" His voice was hesitant.

"Ty? It's Jenny."

No sound.

"Ty?" My voice shook.

"Come in."

I opened the door. He was sitting up in bed with a book in his lap. The little lamp on the bedside table glowed dimly, casting shadows on his muscular arms.

"Can I talk to you for a minute?"

"Uh, yeah, okay." He laid the book on the table.

His gaze met mine, and then he quickly looked away.

I sat down at the foot of the bed. Was I too close? Or too far away? What did he think of me? Maybe he even hated me.

There was a long silence. I traced a star on the leg of my pajamas.

"So," he said.

"So," I repeated. "I thought I would explain to you about Mike."

He nodded.

"Mike and I dated last year. Back when all that stuff was happening with my gift. And we were in a play together. And then the kidnapper guy—he came to the show, and he stabbed Mike in the chest and dragged me away."

Ty's eyes widened in surprise. "What?"

I looked up quickly. "Oh, but it turned out okay. After I kicked the guy in the crotch, the police shot and killed him, so it's all fine."

He raised his eyebrows. "It's all fine?"

"Yeah." I twisted a strand of my hair between my fingers. "Mike survived. Barely. And things were looking very good for us. But then, he went on a boat trip with his family and his Dad's boss, and they convinced him that he shouldn't have a girlfriend during his first year of college."

Ty looked more and more confused.

"So, he broke up with me. And I was a wreck! I mean, I lost it. And then Dad announced that we were going on this crazy boat trip to Alaska and—well, you know the rest."

More silence.

"What are you trying to tell me?"

I bit my lip. "I'm trying to tell you that I didn't have a boyfriend when I met you. So, I wasn't, you know, cheating on him with you."

157

"Okay."

Damn. I couldn't read his expression.

"But then after the summer, you know, you broke up with me."

"Not really," Ty said.

"What?"

"I just said that I wasn't ready for a relationship at the time because I needed to be there for my mom and my aunt."

"Isn't that the same as breaking up?" I frowned. Had I cheated on Ty by making an assumption that wasn't even true?

"I didn't want to end things with you. I just wanted to put them on hold while I sorted things out." I could hear the hurt in his voice.

"But, you didn't call me or text me…" My voice sounded thin.

He sighed. "True. I can see why you would think that."

I looked at him and saw his warm, brown eyes in the soft light. "When I came back from Sitka, Mike was there waiting for me. He apologized for what he had done and wanted me to give him another chance."

"Clearly, you took it." Ty cleared his throat. "Are you happy?"

I shrugged. "I'm taking it very, very slowly with him. But I am happy, yes."

He leaned forward and took my hand. "Then I'm happy for you."

Relief washed over me. "Thank you."

"But, Jenny. There's something else, isn't there?" He looked deep into my eyes. "You have a haunted look about you."

I laughed nervously. "Haunted. That's a great word for it."

Ty gave me a grim look. "Tell me what's been going on here."

A knock startled us and the door swung open.

Our hands broke apart, and I jumped to my feet.

Dad was standing there, looking slightly perturbed. His gaze took in both Ty and me. "You should go to bed, Jenny." He nodded at Ty, his mouth set like granite.

"Yeah, okay." I brushed past my dad, giving Ty a guilty look. "Sorry," I mouthed to him as I scurried down the hall to my room.

I tiptoed across the floor and slid under the cover of my down comforter. Dad looked pissed. How embarrassing. We weren't doing anything. I mean, maybe it looked like we were about to, but… I shuddered. I hoped Ty wasn't too freaked out by my dad.

Cassandra was lying on her back and every now and then, a loud snort escaped her lips.

Ugh. Falling asleep would not be easy.

I rolled onto my side. Ty had said the word "haunted." Was he picking up on all the chaos going on at the theatre? Before our campus visit tomorrow, I would make it a point to tell Ty and Cassandra everything that had been going on since the beginning of the school year. Maybe together we could make some sense of it all.

I tossed and turned, trying in vain to get comfortable enough to sleep. Finally, my body relaxed, and I drifted away.

The blond boy shoved me. "You said you would marry me."

"I know, I know." I shrank back from him. "But I want to finish school."

His cruel laugh broke the silence. "You won't be finishing school. You won't be finishing anything."

I scanned the area, hoping someone, anyone, would come to my defense. But not a single soul was there.

"I told you, you're mine forever. You. Me. We're together forever, do you understand?"

His hand came out of nowhere and struck me hard across the cheek.

My eyes flew open. I could still feel the sting on my face.

"Jenny?" Cassandra's groggy voice called out from her side of the room. "What's wrong?"

I sat up, my heart pounding loudly in my ears.

My phone buzzed on my dresser. It was lit up. Each message said the same thing.

Die.

Die.

Die.

Chapter 28

The next morning, we sat around the table, waiting for Mom to flip the last of the pancakes onto the serving platter.

"I really need to tell you something." I passed a bowl of fruit salad to Jackson.

Mom came in with the pancakes and sat down to join us.

Benny had just arrived and scooted into the empty chair next to me. "What have I missed?"

"Nothing yet." I sipped my coffee.

Ty shifted in his chair. "What's going on, Jenny?"

I leaned forward. "A lot of weird stuff."

"Like what?" Cassandra said with her mouth stuffed with pancakes. It came out more like, "Liewah?"

"It started back in September. I was having a lot of weird dreams about this guy."

Cassandra's eyes got round. "A guy," she repeated. "Is he cute?"

"Uh, I don't know. I guess. But he's not a nice guy. In my dreams, he's very abusive toward his girlfriend. I think he's… evil."

Ty frowned. "This doesn't sound good."

I shook my head. "No, it doesn't. The strange thing is, the dreams aren't in our current time. Everyone in them looks like they're from the 1980s."

"Oh, I love the 80s. Retro is chic, you know?" Cassandra scooped some fruit onto her plate.

Mom stifled a giggle, and then looked guilty for drawing attention away from the subject.

"Besides this guy hurting his girlfriend, what else about these dreams are disturbing?" Ty asked.

"Well, there was this one dream where I was his mom. I had been called to the principal's office. He was expelling her son from school—the blond kid from my dream. At least, I think it was," I said.

"Expelling him for what?" Benny asked.

"For hurting other kids. Beating them up." I pushed a pancake around in the pool of syrup on my plate. "The dream I had last night was of the guy telling his girlfriend that he wanted to marry her."

"That part doesn't sound so bad," Cassandra said.

"But he told her she couldn't finish school—in fact, he said she couldn't finish anything. That there were to be together forever... And then he slapped her."

Benny whistled. "What a piece of work."

I nodded. "Yup. But that's not all of it. At the theatre, there is some serious ghosty stuff going on. And I think the dreams we've been having are related."

Jackson stopped eating and stared at me. "So it's not just a dream? There's a real ghost?"

I told them about the emotion game, when everyone started acting funny. And how I always got the chills during rehearsals. I explained about becoming the rat—and the ghost trying to get me with a knife.

"Don't forget about the tower crashing to the stage and the earthquake in the costume closet," Benny added.

Jackson's mouth hung open. "What?"

"The tower I was in... I watched the nails twisting out of the wood, and it crashed to the stage." I saw the faces of my friends and quickly added, "But don't worry, I wasn't hurt. The earthquake wasn't really an earthquake, but the ghost made the closet shake, and all the costumes fell down on top of me."

"That's some malevolent ghost." Ty looked completely shocked.

"Tell me about it. Honestly, I don't know what to do. I called Celine, but all she said was that I needed to try and reason with the ghost." I swallowed. "You can't reason with this ghost. He's violent."

"Could she come to the theatre and see for herself?" Mom asked. "Maybe she could help."

"Not a bad idea." I gave Mom an appraising look. "I'll call her today."

"Tell them about the other stuff." Benny motioned toward the phone sitting next to my plate. "The texts."

I looked at Mom. "Sorry, I didn't tell you this. I didn't want to scare you."

Mom instantly went rigid in her chair.

"I've been getting some threatening text messages."

"From who?" Ty asked, looking alarmed.

"I don't know. At first, the guy said I was pretty. I thought it was someone from school who maybe had a crush on me. But then, he started saying things like, "'You're mine.' The last texts I got last night all said, 'Die.'"

Mom sucked in a breath. "Oh, my God."

Jackson looked up from his stack of pancakes. "They're related."

"What?" I looked at him blankly.

"The dreams. The ghost. The stalker. They're all related."

My mouth hung open.

Jackson's face was pale. "They're all the same guy."

Chills ran down my spine. "But how could that be? The same—"

The rumble of the school bus echoed through the neighborhood.

"Jackson, the bus!" Mom ran into the kitchen and came back with his lunch bag. "When you come home after school, you're going to have to explain what you meant."

He nodded, still looking shaken.

The grumbling engine got louder.

"Go!" Mom shooed him out the door. She put her hands on her hips and watched him run for the open door of the vehicle. "God. I can't believe this." She turned around and faced us. "I don't know what to say. First my daughter, now my son."

A crumb fell from Cassandra's lips to her plate. She blinked. "OMG. You're both psychic?"

"And Mom too." I tipped my chin toward my mother.

"The whole family?" Cassandra put down her fork.

"Well, yeah, except my dad."

Mom sat down in Jackson's empty chair. "What are we going to do? How could a ghost send threatening text messages?"

I shook my head. "I don't know. But I think it's time we called Celine to see if she can help us figure out what to do—before this ghost kills me."

***

The appointment with Celine was set for four o'clock. There was plenty of time in between for our tour of the University of Washington, which began at nine in the morning.

Mom had signed us in and dropped us off at the Admissions office and had gone to have a cup of coffee at a nearby café.

We met with a tour guide and walked around the campus.

I was still a little worried that we'd run into Mike again, but the campus itself was so big and spread out, I didn't think it was likely.

164

An hour later, we stopped in a large grassy area where the main paths intersected. I knew that in the springtime, the now bare trees would be covered in pale pink cherry blossoms. Students would be sitting on benches, talking, and hoping to catch the first rays of spring sun.

But now the trees were bare. A few crows sat like sentries on the gnarled branches and the clouds were dark with moisture. The smell of rain hung over us like a shroud.

The guide wrapped her arms around herself and crinkled her nose as she looked up at the sky. "Jenny, I'll be taking Ty, Cassandra, and Benny on a tour of the Fine Arts building. Your guide to the School of Drama will pick you up here in just a minute. Do you want us to wait with you?" She squinted at the clouds and shivered.

"No, that's all right. I'll be fine."

She breathed a sigh of relief. "His name is Ray. He'll be here in just a few minutes."

I waved to my friends as they walked quickly to their destination—the tour girl ten feet ahead of them, practically sprinting to get out of the damp, cold air.

My hands dove into the pockets of my down parka. I hoped Ray would get here soon before the sky broke open.

Flash.

The house lights went down.

A spotlight turned on in the center of the stage.

The ghost appeared with a dagger in his hands.

He scanned the audience—a malicious grin parting his bloodless lips.

I held my breath. Did he see me? Did he know I was here?

Like lasers, his eyes found me and fixed on my face.

"There you are. At last."

"Jenny?" A guy put his hand on my shoulder.

I nearly screamed, but struggled to maintain some semblance of composure.

"Are you all right?" The man was in his early twenties. He looked bookish, with a tweed jacket, a plaid scarf, and a pair of dark-rimmed spectacles.

My frantic heart rate stabilized. "Oh, ah, yes. You must be Ray?" I shook his hand. "I guess I was daydreaming."

He laughed. "Maybe you haven't had enough coffee this morning." He motioned toward the path. "I'll take you on a tour of the drama department."

As we walked to the theatre, a boom of thunder rocked the ground, and the clouds burst, sending a wall of water down on us.

Ray nodded to me. "Run!"

***

We dripped puddles onto the lobby floor. My hair hung heavy and wet in my eyes.

"Sorry about that," Ray shook the droplets of water out his hair like a wet dog. "What a day to visit the campus, huh?"

I shivered and took off my rain-soaked coat and wrung it out. "Yeah. I can't believe we got caught in that."

"I'll take you on a tour of the whole facility, but for now, we're in luck. They're rehearsing the first show of the season. I thought you might like to see what a typical rehearsal is like." Ray led me to the auditorium door and opened it. "After you."

It was dark except for the stage. Must have been tech week, since the set was finished and the lighting was perfect.

"They're doing an original production." Ray pointed to a row in the middle of the theatre. "Let's sit there."

We lowered ourselves into the seats as quietly as possible.

"Places!" A voice from a front row seat called—the director.

The actors entered. There was Mike! He was wearing tailored pants and a button-up shirt. His green eyes sparkled in the spotlight.

"This guy is good," Ray whispered to me.

"I know." I leaned forward to watch. As I gazed at Mike, my whole body buzzed with a familiar emotion.

"Oh." He sounded surprised. "You know him?"

"He's my boyfriend." Suddenly, it felt *right* when I said those words. Like my compass had finally found its true north.

Ray gave me a quizzical look. "That's why you want to go to school here?"

"This is one of many schools I'm applying to. But yeah, it would be nice to go to the same university."

Ray shrugged and focused his attention on the stage.

I had made my decision. Last night, I'd let Ty go. I now knew who had my heart.

Mike walked to center stage and sat down on a black chair. The song began in his lower register, soft and sad.

"I thought I'd known love before,
But now I know it wasn't real,
It wasn't 'til you walked through my door
That I knew how love could make me feel."

My senses tingled. Mike didn't realize I was here, but I felt like he was singing directly to me. The tingling sensation in my heart spread to my limbs.

Mike stood up as the song intensified. Now he was in his upper range, and his voice soared out of him like a kite on a windy day.

"And finally you know,
How much I love you.
I would give my soul,
To know you feel the same way I do."

He was better than any Broadway star I'd ever heard. The way he was able to put such emotion into a song. It was a rare gift. When he reached the last note, I stood up, unable to help myself. I whistled and clapped.

Mike shielded his eyes as he looked out into the audience. "Jenny?"

I waved and suppressed the urge to run down the steps of the auditorium and onto the stage. Mike grinned and waved back, a look of astonishment on his face.

Sitting on the edge of my seat, I waited as patiently as I could until the director called for a break. No longer able to contain my enthusiasm, I flew down the stairs, flung my arms around him, and kissed him.

Silence.

Then whoops and laughter from the cast and crew.

I drew back from Mike and gave him an embarrassed smile.

His cheeks were flushed and that crooked grin I found so sexy played on the corners of his lips. "What are you doing here?"

"On a college visit."

He looked past me to the campus guide and out at the empty seats with a furrowed brow. "What about your friends? Cassandra and... Ty?"

A pang of guilt gripped me. "They're with Benny and the other campus guide—checking out the Fine Arts department."

His face clouded for a moment and then he looked back down at me. "I'm glad you came to visit. So, you're applying here for sure?"

"I think so—you know, as a safety school. I'd really rather go to the East Coast."

Mike's hands grasped mine and he pulled me close. "Make sure you tell me where you apply. I'll apply to the same schools as a transfer."

I was shocked. "Seriously? You would do that?"

He wrapped his arms around me. "I told you once that I'd follow you anywhere. I still mean that."

I melted into him.

"Ahem." The director cleared his throat. "Sorry to break up this little reunion, but can we get back to rehearsal? We have a lot of work to do."

"Sorry," Mike and I said at the same time.

I let go of him and climbed back up the stairs. I turned to wave.

He winked at me. "I'll see you at the opening of *Romeo and Juliet.*"

Relief washed over me. And then fear. The ghost was bent on taking me, and whomever was in his way, out.

My phone buzzed in my pocket. "You will all die," the text read.

Chapter 29

We had all assembled on Celine's doorstep—our nervous energy darting between us. I exchanged glances with my posse, and rang the doorbell.

Light footsteps sounded within and the door opened.

Celine welcomed us with her usual smile and open arms. "I didn't expect such a big group."

I hugged her. "I hope that's okay. But there are many of us who want to resolve this issue with the ghost."

"The more the merrier," she quipped. "I think it's wonderful that you have reinforcements."

After we had made introductions and had all taken a seat in her comfortable living room, Celine glanced at all of us. "So, you've all had some sort of dream or vision of this ghost in some form or another, is that right?"

"All except me," Cassandra said. "But I'll help in any way I can."

Celine smiled. "It's good to have help from friends, to be sure. Jackson, your sister told me that you were the one who put this all together. That the ghost is also the one who is sending the menacing text messages?"

Jackson nodded. "I guess I did. I don't know how, but somehow, I just knew."

"He has started developing the same type of gift as Jenny," Mom said.

"It's okay." Celine gave my brother a warm smile. "That's very common. Psychic ability does tend to run in families." Celine got up from her chair. "I'm going to put the tea kettle on. I'll be right back."

"I hope she can help us come up with a plan." Mom gave my hand a squeeze.

"Me too."

Celine returned from the kitchen. "Let's start from the very beginning. Don't leave anything out."

Fifteen minutes later, we had nearly finished summarizing when the kettle began to whistle. Celine disappeared into the kitchen again and reemerged with a tea tray complete with a plate of cookies. She set it down on the coffee table. "Please, help yourselves."

Jackson wolfed down two cookies almost immediately and reached for another. Mom gently put her hand on his arm and he lowered his hand to his lap, looking sheepish.

"So, this morning was when you realized it was the ghost who was also stalking Jenny through threatening text messages." She picked up a cookie from the plate and took a small bite. "I have to tell you, that in all my years of having this gift, I have never, ever heard of such a thing. This entity is extremely powerful. And dangerous."

A prickle of fear ran up my spine. "Yeah, he seems almost more dangerous than a live person. Every time I talk to a guy, he sends me a scary text. It's almost as if he were jealous."

"Oh, he is definitely jealous." Celine took a sip of her tea.

"How can he be jealous, if he doesn't really know Jenny?" Ty asked.

"Good question," Celine answered. "It's possible that Jenny reminds him of someone he loved."

I remembered all the dreams of the blond guy threatening his girlfriend. "I bet I look like her."

"But what is his connection to the theatre?" the psychic asked.

"Not sure. Actually, I have no idea. Except that during some of the visions and dreams, he is dressed like Romeo from *Romeo and Juliet*." I shifted in my seat.

"Hmm. That's the angle then." Celine got up and retrieved her computer from the wooden desk against the wall. "You said the visions take place during the 1980s?"

"The hair and the clothes are a dead giveaway," I said.

"I'm going to visit the theatre's website and see if they have a list of all the plays they've done throughout the years."

"Why didn't I think of that?" I got up and stood behind her while she found the site. "Scroll down to the very end."

"Look at that." Celine pointed to the screen. "1984. *Romeo and Juliet*."

My energy buzzed. I could feel it. "This is why! I'm sure this ghost was in that production, and because I probably look similar to his girlfriend, he thinks I'm her. But what happened to make him want to kill her? I mean, me."

Celine nodded. "You're on the right track, Jenny. Let's find out who this ghost is. Maybe if we learn more about him and what happened during that play, we can find out his motivation."

"And how we can make him stop," Benny added.

"Is there any way to find the cast list from that year?" Mom asked.

"Names aren't listed here." Celine's brow furrowed.

Cassandra raised her hand. "I think I'm about the only person here without super powers, so excuse my ignorance. But, why do psychics need computers to look stuff up?"

We stared at her.

"I mean, shouldn't you just know who the ghost is?" She took another cookie and began munching.

Celine burst into laughter, and we all joined in. "Oh, I like her." She winked at Cassandra.

"It doesn't work that way, Cassandra," I said. "Unfortunately, you don't get the whole universe downloaded into your brain when you're psychic. Maybe we're all different, but I only get bits and pieces of information, and never all at once. I wish it were that easy."

The others nodded.

"But back to our mission. Why don't you try going to the theatre's Facebook page? They have photo albums posted and I've seen some names listed there." I leaned over my mentor's shoulder and watched as she navigated to the page.

She scrolled through the albums until we found the one for 1984. The text below only said the year and the name of the play, but no names were listed.

"There! That's him." I pointed at the photo of the blond guy in the center. He was wearing his Romeo costume. Next to him, wearing a long Renaissance style dress, was a girl with long blond hair.

"She does look like me," I whispered. I wasn't surprised, but it was still chilling to see. Her nose was a bit different and her eyes were more almond-shaped than mine. But still, we looked similar enough. Now I understood why he seemed to be so latched on to me.

The others got up and stood behind Celine who was still sitting on the couch.

"But… why does he keep calling you names and threatening to kill you?" Ty asked. "What happened between the two of them that would make him come after you?"

"That's what we need to find out." I sat back down in my chair. I caught Celine's eye. "Now what?"

"Tell us more." Celine nodded at me. "Think hard. What else has he said in your dreams?"

I chewed on my lip. "Well—he said that I was his forever, oh—and that I'd never be finishing school. In fact, I'd never be finishing anything."

"That goes along with the threats of 'die.'" Benny leaned forward. "What else did he say? Wasn't there something more?"

A sudden memory came back to me. "Yes. He said that I should marry him." Then, a memory from one of my earlier dreams came back to me. "Oh my God."

"What?" Cassandra froze, cookie in mid-air.

"In this one dream, I was sitting in the back seat of a car. *Jack and Diane*, you know that old John Cougar Mellencamp song? It was playing really loud. And you know the part where it goes, "after the thrill of livin' is gone"?

Most of my friends nodded.

"He turned to me and said, 'Do you ever wonder what happens if life doesn't go on? If the thrill of livin' is gone, what's the point?'"

"Does that mean what I think it does?" Jackson asked.

"It means, he wanted to die. And he wanted his girlfriend to die with him." Mom's face paled.

"A suicide pact," Celine whispered.

My body tensed, and I felt the color drain from my face.

"Are you okay, Jenny?" Ty got up and kneeled down beside me.

I took in a deep breath and let it out. "This is all making sense now. The ghost wants to kill me because he and his girlfriend had a suicide pact."

"I'm going to see if I can pull up any information on a 1984 suicide incident." Celine tapped in a quick search on Google. "It's time to arm ourselves with as much information as we can. We can use it to our advantage during the opening night of your show."

174

We crowded around her computer. "There was an incident in 1984 with a teenage boy and girl," she whispered. "An intended double suicide."

"It happened at the theatre—the boy died." Cassandra pointed at the article on the screen.

"What about the girl?" Mom squinted at the monitor, then dug her reading glasses out of her bag.

"She lived," Celine answered.

My fingers tingled. It all made sense.

"The police said that the girl was against the suicide pact from the beginning. But she also had signs of domestic abuse—bruises on her neck, face, and torso. He tried to pressure her into killing herself along with him," Celine said.

My eyes scanned through the words, but couldn't find what I was looking for. "What was the boy's name?"

Celine scrolled through the text. "Chris Babcock."

I remembered my dream where I was the blond boy's mother. The principal had called her Mrs. Babcock. This was it. "Chris Babcock?" I repeated. I pulled up my last text from the stalker. "Cbrj1984."

"Chris Babcock... CB," Benny said. "RJ—*Romeo and Juliet?*"

"1984," Cassandra finished.

I rubbed my temples. Obviously, Caleb Black had never been the CB. It had been Chris Babcock all along. I was so certain the ghost drama and the stalker drama were two separate issues, my mind hadn't let me put the two together. Thank God for Jackson's new ability and my group of friends.

"And now we need to dig a little deeper into this Chris Babcock character," Celine said. "Whatever we can't discover on the internet, we'll have to pool our psychic abilities together to find out the missing pieces."

"Why do we need to do that?" Cassandra looked mystified.

Celine put her hand on Cassandra's arm. "Because we may have to use his background information to help him move on. He needs to cross over."

Jackson rubbed his hands on his jeans. "Do you think he'll try to…hurt us?"

My mentor shrugged. "It's a distinct possibility. That's why we need to learn everything we can to help us fight him. Or at least to convince him that his spite is doing no one any favors."

"I don't know if this is a good idea." Mom's face was ashen. "I don't like the idea of confronting a dangerous ghost with the theatre full of innocent people—my kids included."

Celine directed her gaze toward my mother. "I understand. But this ghost is likely to do something terrible, whether we are prepared or not. He has proven himself agitated enough to cause towers to fall, create earthquakes in closets, and to threaten Jenny's life on numerous occasions. We have to assume that this play—*Romeo and Juliet*—has triggered something in him. A resentment and anger so deep that he will stop at nothing to inflict injury on anyone who happens to be in his path."

"So, you're saying it's inevitable then?" Benny asked.

"Yes, I'm afraid so." Celine turned to my mom. "It's better if we all confront Chris together. There's power in numbers, you know? And we have plenty of people right here to get the job done."

Mom still looked worried. "I guess the problem won't go away unless we meet it head on."

Celine rubbed her hands together. "Let's get to work."

Cassandra's excitement nearly filled the room. "What do we do first?"

"Well," Celine said, "Cassandra, you look up Chris Babcock's parents online—see if they're still alive. Benny, why don't you and Jenny work on finding out about the ghost's girlfriend—her name, where she lives and that sort

176

of thing? Mary, you and Jackson can help me by combing through this article to see if there's anything we've missed."

I bit my lip. "How long will this take? Benny and I need to be at the theatre at six o'clock. It's tech week, and we really can't be late."

Celine glanced at the clock on the wall. "It's four-thirty now. Can you all come back tomorrow?"

"We don't have school on Thursday or Friday—they're teacher in-service days."

"Perfect," Celine said. "Can you be here in the morning around ten?"

I glanced at Mom for approval. She nodded. "I was planning on taking those days off work anyway."

"Okay, go ahead and get a jump on the traffic. I'll see you in the morning."

***

We'd grabbed a take-out dinner on the way back and finished eating at home. Cassandra and Ty stayed with my family while Benny and I dashed out of the house for rehearsal.

"Now I'm more worried than ever." I turned up Gallagher Hill on Mercer Island.

Benny rummaged around in the bag on his lap. "Celine gave me a little vial of holy water."

I scrunched up my face. "What're we supposed to do with that?"

"She said that once your costume is on, sprinkle it all over yourself. I already sprinkled it on me since I don't have to wear a costume."

"Will it work?"

"I guess it couldn't hurt. Celine said that it works with some ghosts, but not all. Also, leave a little in the bottle in case you have to throw it on him—you know, if he attacks you or something."

My stomach churned. "This whole thing is making me really nervous."

Benny patted my leg. "It's going to be okay. You're not in this alone."

We pulled into the parking lot with a minute to spare.

"Thanks, Benny. We'll see you in there." I ran for the backstage door and signed myself in. I prayed that Chris Babcock would leave me alone.

***

After the first hour of rehearsal, Jack announced that we were to take a break in the lobby while the crew fixed some things on the set.

The men with the measuring tapes were back. I could feel the tension from the staff and the actors. We all knew why they were there.

"They could at least come during the daytime when we didn't have to see them," Miguel muttered under his breath.

One of the men shot him a harsh look. "Sorry, but we're on a tight deadline."

"But we're putting on a show." Ross stepped forward and glared at the man. "It ruins our creative energy when we're reminded that you're tearing down our theatre."

"Ross—" Miguel pulled him back a few steps. "You have to remember that the school district is only doing their job. However, these *men* they hired don't have to be so rude about it."

The man shook his head, and he and his cohort walked through the lobby and down the hall to the back of the building.

Cold air seeped past us.

"Can you make sure the front doors are shut tightly?" Miguel said to Caleb. "There's a draft in here."

"Do you feel that?" Benny nudged me.

178

"Yeah." I stuck my hand in the pocket of my dress, feeling the vial of holy water there.

The frigid air floated through the lobby and minutes later, we heard the men exclaim. "What the hell?" There was a loud thump, and then a series of muffled expletives.

The men came hurrying back to the lobby, rubbing their heads. A red bump was forming on the forehead of the tall man.

"Look," the shorter man said angrily, "I know you guys are upset about the building, but there's no reason to rig up those boxes so they'd fall on us. We could report you to the police if we wanted to."

"What?" Miguel's mouth hung open.

"Don't play dumb with me," the taller man said. "Those boxes literally flew across the room at us. Obviously, you've set this whole thing up."

I'd never seen Miguel so angry.

"How dare you?" he said. "You waltz in here, unannounced—we didn't even know you were coming, by the way, and then accuse us of planning some kind of cheap prank? If anyone should be calling the police, it should be us. You guys are nuts!"

The men scowled at him. "We'll be sure to let the school district know about your little trick. I'm sure it will help negotiate your early eviction."

Miguel's eye twitched. "You—"

But before he could get out any further insults, a low rumble rippled through the floor.

"Is that an earthquake?" Madeline grabbed onto Caleb's arm.

Icy air blasted through the lobby.

"And turn down the goddamn air conditioning," the shorter man said. "Don't you people know it's November?"

"We don't have air conditioning. It's been broken for years, you idiot," Miguel snarled. "Now, get out. You're disrupting our rehearsal."

The actors cheered, and the men stomped out.

"Don't let the door hit you in the butt on the way out," Ross called.

I leaned over to whisper in Benny's ear. "Never thought I'd say this, but, that's one time I'm glad there's a badass ghost here."

The auditorium doors swung open. "Okay, the lights are set, and we've fixed the movable wall. Let's start at the top of Act Two," Jack said.

The students were still whispering about the jerks when they took their places on stage.

"Quiet down, guys." Jack clapped his hands. "Let's not forget why we're all here."

Backstage, my hands shook as I smoothed the folds of my Juliet costume. The ghost of Chris Babcock was getting bolder and bolder. It was a wonder that no one else had caught on to the fact that there was a very angry ghost in residence in this theatre.

There were two more days until opening night. Would we be able to stop him before he hurt anyone else?

Chapter 30

We knocked on Celine's door. The two boxes of doughnuts I held felt heavy in my arms. I shrugged my shoulder, trying to keep the laptop bag's strap from digging into it. At least I wasn't carrying the Joe-to-go boxes of Starbucks like Benny and Ty. I could see the angry, red grooves made from the cardboard handle cutting into their hands. Parking close to your destination was sometimes challenging in downtown Seattle.

The door opened. "Welcome!" Celine rushed forward and hugged each of us, careful not to knock any supplies out of our arms. She led us into her comfortable living room, and we unloaded our loot onto the coffee table.

We spent the next fifteen minutes eating carbs and drinking coffee. Once we were full and caffeinated, Celine cleared her throat. "Let's go over a few things before we get started."

"Jenny, I think it would be great if we could get into the theatre before everyone shows up for the performance. Is that possible?"

"I… don't know." Oh my God. I would have to ask either the stage manager, Miguel, or Jack, the director. They might just think I'm crazy.

Celine must've sensed my distress. "Why don't you all start on the tasks I assigned you. Jenny, can I talk to you for a moment?" She gestured toward the kitchen.

I got up and followed her.

The kitchen was a light, buttery yellow color. Sunshine flooded the room from the windows. A small dining table stood in the corner. Her apartment always put me at ease. We got settled in the white dining chairs.

"I wanted to talk to you a little bit before we dive in."

I wiped my hands on my jeans. "What's up?

Her face softened and the light streaming in from the windows seemed to create a halo effect around her. "I know this has been difficult for you. With the threatening text messages, and the antics at the theatre—I can understand why you'd be agitated and stressed. Is there something more bothering you? Something I can help you with?"

She had no idea. I was living in a constant state of stress. Between the ghost stalker and being confused as to which guy I wanted to date, I was a train wreck. Thank God I had realized that Mike was who I wanted to be with. At least that was one less thing to stress about.

"You're right. I'm frazzled. Like, all the time. I feel like I'm being watched and threatened 24/7 for the last couple of months. So, when you asked if I could get us into the theatre early—it pushed me into a panic." I twisted my hair between my fingers. "I'm scared."

"Of the ghost?"

"No. I mean, yes. But I'm also scared of telling the people at the theatre about all this psychic stuff."

Celine gave me a patient look, waiting for me to elaborate.

I got up and began to pace. "I've come a long way since that first time we met—when we had to find Callie, the missing girl from my school. Back then, I didn't want to acknowledge that I was psychic, even to myself. I didn't want to be different. But I've come to terms with my gift, and I know I'm supposed to use it to help people."

"But?"

I let out a burst of air. "I still don't want to expose my gift to everyone! I mean, if I go tell the people at YTN that I need to get into the theatre early so I can rid the theatre of an evil ghost, they're…"

"Going to think you're crazy?" Celine filled in.

"Yes!" I could feel my face getting warm. "There. I've said it. They'll think I'm crazy."

Celine laughed and then realized that maybe it was inappropriate. "I'm not laughing at you, really I'm not. But this is all bringing back memories of my own journey of being psychic. I used to be just as horrified as you are that I was different. It's hard to believe, but eventually you'll come to a point when you just don't care what other people think. I'd almost forgotten how self-conscious teenagers are."

I sat back down. "I can't wait to get to that point in my life. To be comfortable in my own skin… that would be awesome."

"You'll get there someday, I promise." Her smile lit up her face. "In the meantime, pick one person at the theatre that you think would be the most understanding of your request. Which person on the staff would be most likely to help us? Is there anyone who has seen or felt the ghost there?"

I mentally scrolled through the list of adults at the theatre. There was Jack, but I didn't think he was the right person to approach. He was great, but I was a tiny bit intimidated by him. There was the fight choreographer, but I'd seen him take the boys down a couple of notches when they got out of hand. But then I thought about Miguel. He had been there when the tower crashed to the stage. And, he'd heard the boxes being thrown at the men with the measuring tapes when they'd interrupted our rehearsal. I had a glimmer of hope that he wouldn't think I was crazy. In fact, he might welcome an opportunity to stop all the strange and dangerous stuff happening in the theatre.

"Miguel," I said.

"Miguel is?"

"The stage manager. I have a sense he might be the most likely to believe me."

"Perfect. Why don't you give him a call?"

I took a deep breath. "Okay."

"Do you want me to step out of the room?" Celine asked.

I shook my head. "No. It would be great if you could stay." I took out my phone and scrolled through my contacts. My finger hovered over the number. Why was it still so hard for me to let people know about my gift?

Celine gave me a reassuring look. "When you're ready."

I pushed the number. It rang. My heart beat faster.

"Hello?"

I could hear my pulse pounding in my ears. I put it on speaker phone so Celine could hear too. "Miguel? It's Jenny."

"Oh, hi. Is everything all right? Are you going to be late for tech today?"

"No, I'll be on time. I wanted to ask you if I could get into the theatre early on Friday. Does the Mercer Island school district also have today and Friday off?"

"Yup," he answered.

"I was hoping you'd say that. May I bring in a few people before the theatre opens—say around three o'clock?" I looked at Celine and she nodded. Three hours should be enough time to deal with the ghost, I hoped.

"A group of people?" Miguel sounded confused.

"Miguel, I don't know if you'd noticed, but there are some strange things going on there as of late."

"Strange things… like the stuff about the sword fighting and the boxes being tossed at the men who were in to take measurements?"

So, he did notice. "Yes."

"What do those things have to do with the group of people you want to bring in?"

"Well, most people don't know this about me, but…" I drew in a deep breath. "I'm psychic."

"What?"

Oh, geez. "I'm psychic."

There was a prolonged moment of silence on his end. My gaze flicked over to Celine. She reached out and patted my arm.

"Yeah. And so I've had a lot of stuff happen to me at the theatre—paranormal things. I don't know what your thoughts are on this, but we have a ghost at YTN."

"Ghost." Miguel echoed.

"Do you believe in that sort of thing?"

"Actually, I sort of do," Miguel said. "I think one of my great aunts had some kind of psychic ability. My family talks about it every now and then. I agree. There a few things that have happened lately which have made me wonder."

Okay, good, I wasn't getting resistance from him.

"Before opening night, I'd like to see if we can get the ghost to leave—to cross over or whatever, so we don't have any more dangerous things happening. Especially with an audience there."

"And these people are?"

"Friends of mine that have a similar ability. In fact, I have three people with me right now that have experience with this sort of thing."

"Only four of you, then?" Miguel asked.

"No, I have several others, including my mom and brother, who will be helping too."

"Well, I guess that would be all right. I can meet you at YTN and open the doors for you. I'll need to stick around though."

"That's fine. We should be done by the time the cast and crew arrive at six o'clock. Hopefully."

"Let's hope it works," he said. "I've got to go now, but I'll see you at three o'clock tomorrow."

I pushed the end call button on my screen and blew out a breath.

"You did it!" Celine grinned.

"I did. It wasn't as bad as I thought it would be."

"People are generally more accepting to these sorts of things than you'd think, right?" She got up and pushed her chair in.

I followed suit and pushed mine in as well. "Thank God for that."

When we entered the living room, I joined Benny, who was sitting on the floor in front of my laptop which was open on the coffee table. Mom and Jackson were huddled around her laptop, and Cassandra was focused on the computer that Jackson brought.

I leaned into Benny. "Find anything out about Chris's girlfriend?"

He nodded. "I think I found her."

"She's alive then?"

"Yes, and living right here in Seattle." He turned the screen to toward me and pointed.

I gasped. "That's four blocks from here."

"I know."

***

"How is everyone coming along with their assignments?" Celine asked. "Can you share what you've learned?"

"I found Chris's girlfriend." Benny pointed to the laptop screen. "Her name is Tanya Larson, and wait for it… she lives within walking distance."

"That's quite a coincidence, don't you think?" Celine winked and then said, "I don't believe in coincidences.

We'll definitely address this after we've heard from everyone else."

Cassandra went next. "I found out that Chris's mom died of cancer a few years after her son died."

"And his dad?" Celine asked.

"He moved to Wisconsin and got remarried," Cassandra said. "So neither one of them can be much help."

"Not true," Celine said. "The mother will be very helpful to us."

"But I just told you she's dead." Cassandra's brows furrowed.

"Yes, and that's why she can be helpful. We have enough psychic energy in this room to talk to any spirit we like—if she wants to be heard."

"Oh." Cassandra's voice buzzed with excitement. "Are we going to have a séance?"

Celine laughed. "Well, I guess you could call it that. We can use our energy to summon her. I think she has much to tell us about her son."

"It may be that she's already tried," my mom said.

I remembered the dreams we'd both had about the ghost's mom arguing with her son, and the one about Chris getting expelled from school.

"Yeah, that's true," I said. "I think she was trying to tell us that she tried her best with him."

"Do you think he was mentally ill?" Benny asked.

"It could be." Celine sat down on the couch. "It's one explanation for his irrational desire to kill his girlfriend."

"Very true." I chewed on my lip.

"Let's see what she has to tell us." Celine stood up and opened a drawer in the large, antique bureau against the wall. The top of it was a shrine or altar of sorts, displaying a large vase filled with purple and white flowers, bird feathers, gold coins, candles, and an assortment of stones. She took out a book of matches, closed the drawer, and came back with a large white candle on a silver tray. She went back and collected a cross pendant, some incense, and a few purple flowers.

She lit the incense, which instantly filled the room with a pungent, smoky odor mixed with the scent of herbs I couldn't begin to identify. Next, she lit the candle. "Come, everyone sit and join hands."

Cassandra practically threw herself on the floor near Celine with her hands stretched out.

I smiled, sat down next to her, and took her hand. I was expecting Ty to sit next to me, but instead, my little brother scooted himself into position and held my hand. It was sweaty.

"Are you all right?" I asked him.

He looked scared. "I guess so."

"Don't worry, I'm here. Mom's here—it'll be fine."

"Cassandra, what's Mrs. Babcock's first name?" Celine asked.

"Rachel."

Celine sang a beautiful hymn which honored God, the angels, and all the helping spirits from the other side. She then asked that the spirit of Chris's mother, Rachel, come forward.

Nothing.

She asked again.

When the silence continued, she said, "We want to help your son, Rachel. He needs you."

The candle flickered.

I shivered.

The flame went sideways, back and forth.

"Rachel?" Celine said.

White haze gathered in the middle of our circle and soon formed into the shape of a woman. She wasn't very well-defined, but she definitely had a feminine presence.

"I'm here," the spirit whispered.

Jackson gasped. The rest of us had seen spirits, animal spirits, and even angels. I wasn't sure what my mom had seen in her lifetime. But Jackson had never seen anything like this before.

I squeezed his hand. "It's okay."

"Rachel." Celine smiled. "Thank you for coming. Your son, Chris, is causing great fear and danger among the living."

"Yes," Rachel said. "I know. I'm sorry."

"It's not your fault," Celine continued. "Tomorrow, we'll try to help him make the transition. May we ask for your assistance?"

The haze shifted. Rachel's face became more in focus. Her eyes looked almost watery. "I don't know that I can help. He never listened to me in life."

"I think he did," Celine said. "He only chose to ignore you. This time, I think he'll pay attention."

"Why now?"

"Because he hasn't seen you in a very long time." Celine held out her hands in an open gesture. "He's very alone. Again, it's a choice he has made, but we need him to realize that his choices have only brought him sadness. If we can show him that there is an alternative—to accept peace and love—he will perhaps choose to move on. Then you can be together."

"I will be there if he chooses to cross over. But I cannot force him to do so. It has to be his decision, not mine." Rachel's form broke apart and dissolved until only particles of dust were visible in the glow of the candle.

We unclasped our hands, processing her appearance in silence.

Finally, Celine stood up. "Jenny, you and Benny know what you have to do next, right?"

"Go see Chris's girlfriend?" My heart started pounding harder just thinking about it.

"Yes."

"She'll think we're crazy." Benny gave me a worried look.

My eyes met Celine's. "It's a risk we'll have to take." I knew there was a possibility that Tanya would throw us out of her home—or maybe not even let us in to begin with. But when I'd told Miguel about our plan to rid the theatre of the ghost, he had been more understanding than I thought. So why not Tanya?

"Okay." Benny didn't sound very certain.

"What's the worst that could happen?" I asked Benny as we left Celine's apartment.

"She could call the police." Benny closed the door behind us.

"Let her," I said. "If she calls the police, we'll just leave. Besides, Detective Coalfield can smooth things over if for some reason they catch up to us."

"Ha! I hadn't thought of that." He stopped in the hall. "Wait a minute. We should call her before we go over."

"You're right." I pulled out my phone. I'd put her number into my contacts list earlier.

"What are you going to say?" Benny asked.

"Nothing right now. If she answers, we'll know she's home. It's better to talk face to face." I touched the number on the screen.

"Hello?" a woman's voice said.

I hung up. "She's home."

***

The clouds covered the sun and it began to drizzle. In the next moment, patches of blue sky peeked out, and then it was back to gray again. Typical for early November.

"What do you think she's going to do when she realizes why we're at her door?"

"Well," I said, "there's only one way to find out."

We reached her building and waited for the elevator in the lobby. I pushed the button for the fourth floor.

My palms were sticky and my mouth went dry.

Benny reached out to push the doorbell on number 404. "Ready?"

"As I'll ever be."

He pushed the button. A little dog yipped a frantic bark somewhere within the apartment. Then we heard footsteps. My heart thudded in my chest.

"Just a minute! Skipper, be quiet!"

I turned to look at Benny.

He gave me a reassuring smile. "It'll be all right."

The door opened a crack, a chain keeping it from opening completely. "Yes? Can I help you?" the woman's voice said. Skipper continued to yip.

"Hi." I rubbed my hands on my jeans. "Sorry to bother you. I'm Jenny Crumb and this is my friend Benny. We're doing a production of *Romeo and Juliet* at Youth Theatre Northwest, and we understand that you were in the 1984 production?"

I held my breath.

She undid the chain. "Youth Theatre Northwest." Her voice took on an odd inflection. I couldn't interpret if she sounded wistful or scared. "Come in," she said softly.

The door swung open. She was about my height. I figured she was forty-seven or forty-eight years old, and I thought she looked good for her age. Her blond hair was pulled into a bun, and a pair of black-rimmed reading glasses were perched on her nose.

Benny and I followed her inside. The apartment was small and sparsely decorated.

"Have a seat." She motioned toward the floral sofa situated under the window. The light streamed onto the yellow flowers of the fabric, giving them a cheery look which almost seemed out of place, given the circumstances.

I felt a lump in my throat as I tried to swallow. "So…"

"Youth Theatre Northwest." She tried a smile. "I haven't thought of that place in years. I can't believe it's still there."

191

"Actually, it won't be for long. At least the building won't—it's being torn down."

"Oh!" She looked sad and then relieved.

"It's moving to a temporary space while the new performing arts center is being built," Benny interjected.

"I see." She put her little dog down and he jumped up on the couch between Benny and me.

His fluffy, black fur and his bubblegum pink tongue made him look like a stuffed animal. "He's so cute." I ran my hand down his back and scratched his butt. He wiggled it with glee.

"Thanks. He's been great company after my divorce."

"Animals are great," I said, and then realized how dumb that sounded.

"So, you two are here because…"

I rubbed my hand across my face. "Because." Ugh, this was going to sound ridiculous. "Because, there are some really strange things happening at the theatre—and we think you might be able to help with that."

"Excuse me?" Tanya's little dog jumped onto her lap and settled down. "I don't know what you mean."

Benny and I exchanged a glance. I took a deep breath. "I mean, there's a ghost in the theatre."

Now she looked even more confused.

"Let's back up a little," Benny said. "I know this will seem strange, and you might not even believe us, but Jenny is psychic. And so am I."

I jumped in before she could respond. "And there's been a lot of weird stuff happening at the theatre. We have… reason to believe that your ex-boyfriend, Chris Babcock, is the ghost who is causing all the trouble."

A look of complete shock crossed Tanya's face. "What?" She stood up. The little dog scampered off the arm chair and sat looking up at her.

I stood up too. "I'm so sorry. I know this is bizarre. We wouldn't have come here if we didn't think you could help us. But this ghost is targeting me. I play Juliet—and that's the part that you had, isn't it?"

She stared at me.

"Ever since rehearsals have started, I've been feeling cold air around me. I've had strange dreams of a high school boy threatening me, and saying things like, 'we'll be together forever,' and calling me names like 'slut' and 'whore.'"

She gasped and sat back down in the chair. The dog jumped back onto her lap.

"The ghost, Chris, is getting more and more violent." I sat back down. "He made Juliet's tower, with me in it, crash to the stage."

"He made an earthquake happen in the costume closet," Benny added. "And threw boxes at some construction guys from the school district."

She leaned back on the couch and looked deflated. "Sounds like Chris."

"His behavior and his strength are escalating," I said. "Tomorrow is opening night. I'm afraid he's going to try to hurt me and a lot of other people. We have to stop him."

"But why would he do that?" Her voice was tiny, like a little girl's.

"Why did he do any of the things he did to you back in 1984?"

"He was sick." Tanya shook her head. "Normal people don't try to convince a teenage girl to kill herself. He *scared* me."

"I know. I had a bunch of dreams where I was you. And the things he said to you…"

"Why would I go back there? He'll try to kill me." She shrank back into the couch.

So, she really believed us then. That was a good first step. "Because you can help him to cross over to the other side; help him to be at peace."

"You really think he's going to go to *heaven*?" She shook her head. "He terrorized me. He hit me. He threatened me every single day. I don't think a guy like that is meant to go to heaven."

I shrugged. "I honestly don't know where he will go. All I know is that he does need to leave the theatre. We believe that he was psychotic. At the very least, he was unstable. I hope that when he crosses over, he will find peace. He's stuck between this world and the next. Our goal is to get him to go wherever he's supposed to go."

She crossed her arms. "And who is this 'we' you speak of? You two? I hardly think two teenagers will be able to get him to leave if he hasn't gone anywhere for thirty years."

I cleared my throat. "Believe it or not, we have a team of people to help—most of them are psychic like us. Celine, my mentor, has experience with this sort of thing. She's certain we can get him to go."

"If you have a team of people, why do you need me?" She frowned.

"You might be the key. If he can see that you're alive— and that you're not *me*, maybe he will come around and realize the truth."

She said nothing for several minutes.

Benny nudged me. "We should go," he whispered.

I sighed and stood up. "Thank you for inviting us in. I'm sorry we bothered you."

"Wait." Tanya motioned for us to sit back down. "I'll do it."

"Really?" I couldn't believe it.

"Part of me wants to kick you both out and pretend you were never here."

"And the other part?" Benny asked.

"The other part wants me to deal with this problem head on. After Chris killed himself, I kind of lost it. It was devastating. Kids whispered about me, called me a murderer—as if I had killed him. I don't even know how I

194

got through the rest of the school year. Somehow, I managed to keep my sanity. My parents really should've had me go to a therapist, but they didn't believe in that sort of thing. They encouraged me to forget all about it; to move on with my life. So, I did. My life was normal on the surface, but I've struggled emotionally ever since." Her laugh had a bitter edge to it.

"Do you think facing Chris will help you?" Benny sat forward and looked her in the eye. "Maybe it will be therapeutic or something."

"Perhaps I do need closure." She looked away. "It's odd that you showed up at a time like this. With my divorce still being a fresh wound."

"Celine, the woman I was telling you about? She doesn't believe in coincidences," I offered. "Maybe the timing is perfect."

Chapter 31

I spent over an hour curling my long hair and adding a few delicate braids to make it look like I had stepped out of the Renaissance period. I carefully applied my stage makeup and generously applied powder to set it. I had no idea how long it would take to rid the theatre of the ghost, so I wanted to be ready for opening night in case I didn't have time to come back home.

The drive there was mostly silent—we were all apprehensive about facing a supernatural entity, and had no idea what to expect.

Dark clouds hung overhead as we pulled into the parking lot. It smelled like rain.

Miguel was waiting by the front doors. He unlocked them as we approached. In total, we had seven people ready to help. I was crossing my fingers that Tanya would show up soon—and she would make eight people. As far as I was concerned, the more the merrier. I was just glad I didn't have to face the ghost on my own.

Celine was taking supplies out of her trunk. She joined us in the lobby, carrying bundles of sage and white candles.

"What are those for?" Jackson asked. He'd been really quiet throughout this whole ordeal. I wondered if he was too scared to go through with this.

"We use sage to clear the spirits from homes and buildings." Celine handed him a ceramic bowl and a bundle of sage. "It cleanses the space too, so they won't come back when we're done."

"At least, I hope they don't," I muttered. Even if Chris did come back, the building would be torn down soon. He wouldn't have any place to come back to. Where did ghosts go when their favorite places to haunt were torn down?

Celine took several bottles of holy water out of the car and began handing them out. "We'll begin by dipping our fingers in the water and painting each door and window with the sign of the cross."

"Does holy water really work?" Ty asked.

"This isn't just any holy water. This is from Lourdes, France. I grew up Catholic, and it's something that my mom told me about a long time ago. It's the most powerful holy water there is."

"What makes it so powerful?" Jackson asked.

"The Virgin Mary appeared to a woman who lived in Lourdes, back in the 1800s. It is said that the water can heal people—I guess you could say it's miracle water. People still flock to Lourdes to bathe in the spring water there, hoping for miracles of their own."

"But what can it do for us?"

"I believe that anything with powerful spiritual properties can protect us against evil," Celine said. "And it's worked for me so far. I've rid dozens of ghosts from people's homes, and have helped them cross over in this way."

"Even angry ones?" Mom asked.

My mentor laughed. "Yup, even angry ones. Oh, the stories I could tell."

"Maybe save those for after," Cassandra said. "I'm super into this." She picked up a bottle of holy water, uncorked it and sniffed. "It doesn't smell like anything."

"Because it's water, dummy." Benny nudged her.

"Oh, yeah. Duh." Cassandra giggled and put the cork back in.

Miguel watched all of this in fascination. "What's the game plan?"

Celine had piled all of the supplies in the corner. She opened a bag of white candles and handed one to each of us. "First, we're going to pray. This will be more powerful if we all sing together."

Miguel, who was also holding a candle, cleared his throat. "Do you want me to join in?"

"We can use all the positive energy we've got. The hymn goes like this:

We ask you, God
To protect us all
From darkness.
Surround us with
Thy healing light
And keep us safe
Within your loving embrace."

Next, Celine led us through a series of protection prayers, all meant to surround us with white light and to keep out dark or negative energy. I was hoping to get a little more comfort from them, but I had a weird feeling about what might happen in the next few hours.

Finally, we were done. I looked at the time on my phone. It was three-thirty. Two and a half more hours until the cast arrived. Despite the fact that the students weren't in the building, the staff definitely was. The technical director was busy in the auditorium, cleaning up the construction mess and putting finishing touches on the set before the opening night performance.

"Let's save the auditorium for last," Celine said. "It's the largest space and will take all of us working together to clear it."

"What do we do now?" Cassandra asked.

"Let me show you." Celine led us outside. She opened a ceramic bottle with a cross painted on the outside. She poured a little on her fingers and then painted a cross on each glass door. "We need to do this on every door of the building."

We divided into two groups, each group with a bottle. It didn't take long to finish all the doors.

"Next, we're going to break into groups, and cleanse every room with sage. When we get to the auditorium, we'll all go in together."

"Why can't we do the whole thing as a group?" My eye started to twitch.

Everyone turned their attention toward me.

I pushed my index finger to the site of the twitch and held it down. "I mean, it seems as though there's power in numbers, right?" And also, I thought, the ghost had very specifically told me on many occasions that he would kill me.

"Because he can escape us if we chase him as a group. There will always be an exit for him to get away." Celine tugged on the bundle of sage in her hand. "If we divide into groups, we can herd him toward the auditorium, where we can converge on him together."

I reluctantly agreed. "I guess that makes sense."

After instructions from Celine, Benny, Cassandra, Ty and I started our ritual in the back of the theatre, while the other group began in the front of the building.

I opened the doors to the Studio Stage, the small black box space where the ghost had scared us on Halloween. The hair stood up on the back of my neck. I had a bad feeling about this.

We turned on the lights and each lit a bundle of sage in ceramic bowls. We dipped our herbs in the bowls to put out the flames and then let them smolder. The smoky tendrils wandered lazily around our group. I stifled a cough as it curled around my face. Starting in the middle of the room, we let the smoke fan out while we said phrases like, "God and the angels command you to go the light," and "The white light surrounds and fills this space with goodness and positive energy."

Each of us took a corner of the room and filled it with the smoke of the sage. Then, we did the same procedure on the small stage, the wings, and the room behind the stage. The floor groaned.

"What was that?" Ty asked.

"I don't know." I fanned some smoke behind the curtain. "This is an old building. It could've been anything." I was trying to make myself feel better as much as I was trying to put everyone at ease.

We walked out of the black box and headed into the hall to continue with the cleansing. Cold air raised goosebumps on my arms. "Do you feel that?"

Cassandra squeaked and moved closer to me. "Should I go get Celine?"

I looked around nervously. Celine and the rest of the group had started in the lobby. They would be working their way back here anytime now. "Not yet. We should try to get as much done as we can. Let's go sage the Blue Room."

I gave one more glance down the hall, and could see the others fanning smoke through the front half of the building. I hoped they would hurry up and join us. Doubt crept into my mind.

We entered the Blue Room and turned on the lights. I lit a new bundle of white sage and smudged out the sparks in the bowl. The herbs smoldered, and the burned odor wafted up into the air around us. The smell was a combination of burnt Thanksgiving turkey and the charred odor of fields burned after harvest. Cassandra, Benny, and Ty did the same, and we split up to cover all the areas.

"I almost forgot about the snack room." This was where the preschool drama classes had snacks and did messy art projects. I opened the door which led to the small room lodged between the Blue Room and the Studio Stage.

A blast of icy air hit me in the face, lifting the hair off my shoulders. I stumbled backward.

Ty rushed forward and caught me in mid-fall.

My phone buzzed in my pocket. Dread hit me like a punch to the gut. Both the door to the hallway and the one to the snack room slammed shut. Benny and Cassandra ran to rattle the door knobs. They were locked.

We turned to look at each other. I slowly pulled the phone out and looked at the screen.

"Time to die," it read.

I swallowed a scream.

A look of alarm crossed Ty's face. "What does it say?"

I held the phone out to him.

He read the text. "Oh, Jenny."

Benny and Cassandra rushed to my side to look at the message.

"Oh my God!" Cassandra shrieked. She ran back to the door and put all her weight against it as she tried to turn the knob.

"Help!" Benny yelled at the top of his lungs.

Ty ran to Cassandra's side and began pushing against the door with all his might.

A hissing noise filled the room, and the chairs that were lined up against the walls began to tremble. The temperature dropped at least ten degrees, and the cold air swirled around us. My hair whipped around my head.

The hissing noise grew louder, accompanied by a low rumbling under our feet—as though it were bubbling up from the depths of hell.

We covered our ears as the sound increased.

"What should we do?" Ty shouted.

I only knew what he was saying by reading his lips. My mind went blank.

Then I remembered the protection prayers that Celine had taught me. I motioned for the rest of the group to huddle together. I reached my hands out. "Hold hands, everyone!"

201

I wasn't sure if they had heard me. I grabbed Ty's hand and then Cassandra's. She caught on and reached for Benny.

Soon we were joined in a small circle, shivering with the cold.

"The light of God surrounds us. The love of God enfolds us. The power of God protects us!" I shouted as loud as I could. "The light of God surrounds us. The love of God enfolds us. The power of God protects us!"

The others caught on and joined in. The noise lessened a bit, but the cold was still there.

I saw panic in each of my friends' eyes. What could I do to protect them from this entity?

"Leave them alone!" I pulled away from the circle. My friends were in danger because of me. Because this *thing* was intent on bringing me down. "Let them go!" I shouted even louder. "They've done nothing to you. Take me and let them go."

The sound died down a little more.

"Jenny!" My mom yelled from the hall. "Open the door!"

I ran to the door and twisted the knob. Still locked. "I can't. Get Celine! The ghost is in here with us."

"I'm here," Celine called out. "Hang on, Jenny. Miguel is getting the key."

"I don't think that'll work." I shoved the door with my shoulder. Just then, I heard a key being slipped into the lock. The knob rattled.

"It won't open," Miguel said.

The wind picked up again. A chair flew through the air and crashed against the opposite wall.

"Do something!" I yelled.

"I'll get a screwdriver. We're going to take this door off the hinges."

"Hurry." Benny clung to me.

It was so cold now, my hands were turning blue and I couldn't feel the tips of my fingers.

Celine began chanting protection prayers on the other side of the door, but it only seemed to infuriate the ghost. The windows rattled. The floor shook harder.

I looked at my friends' terrified faces. Was this the last time I would ever see them? I pulled them all close to me and we wrapped our arms around each other.

Another chair flew across the room and came dangerously close to hitting me. Cassandra let out a yelp and threw her arms over her head, trying to shield herself from the onslaught.

Noises from the hall grew louder. Celine was nearly shouting prayers and mantras. The sound of metal against metal tipped me off that Miguel had arrived and was taking the hinges off.

Just as the door was wrenched open, the wind died, and the hissing and rumbling stopped. It was dead silent.

Chapter 32

We spilled out of the Blue Room and into the hall, too shocked to utter even a single word.

Cold air blasted past us and down the long hallway.

"He's headed to the auditorium." Celine grabbed my arm and pulled me along.

"How do you know?" Ty hurried to keep up with us.

"Because we've already saged the rest of the building," Celine said. "There's nowhere else he can go. Come on, hurry."

We reached the auditorium in seconds. Miguel pulled the doors open.

John, the technical director stood by the stage, looking confused and cold. "What's going on? Did someone fix the air conditioning?"

The drop in temperature was bone chilling. I shivered, not only with the cold, but with sheer terror.

Celine turned to me. "Jenny, I have to apologize to you. I didn't realize how powerful this ghost is." She shook her head. "I didn't take you seriously enough. Had I known this would happen, I would've brought reinforcements."

Great. Wish she had thought of that earlier.

Ty ran his fingers through his hair. "Now that we have him trapped here, what do we do? Is he too strong for us?"

Celine grimaced. "I'm not going to lie. In all my years of doing this, I have never, ever seen an entity so violent… and capable of doing this much harm."

My stomach lurched. So, not only was I terrified, but my mentor—who I was sure had seen and done just about everything in the paranormal realm, was not sure she could handle our evil incarnate ghost. She seemed almost as scared as I was.

The cold wind was intensifying. The stage curtains fluttered with the waves of air circulating the theatre.

John, the technical director, pushed his glasses up on his nose. "What's going on? Where is this cold air coming from?"

Miguel took him aside and began to explain in low whispers.

John's expression, first amused, changed to a look of astonishment. "You mean, a ghost is behind all the weird stuff that's been happening here the last couple of months?"

So, he had noticed it too. Like most people, he'd probably written it off as coincidence. But no one could ignore what was happening right now in this theatre.

The floor rumbled.

I grabbed Celine's arm. "Now what?" The panicky feeling I'd had throughout the day intensified.

Celine's face was set in stone. "Now we make him leave."

"How?" Cassandra looked like she was about to faint.

"Join hands." Celine grasped Cassandra's hand and then mine. "Quickly, in a circle, everyone."

I nodded toward Miguel and John to join us. Miguel grabbed Cassandra's hand, but John lagged behind.

"I don't know." John looked apprehensive. "This is pretty weird. I'm not into this kind of stuff."

"It doesn't matter if you're into it or not," Celine said. "Just do it."

A piece of half-painted plywood flew off the side of the stage and came hurtling toward us. John ducked and reached out his hands. Benny and I grabbed his hands and watched the board sail into the seats behind us.

"You too. Quickly!" Celine nodded her head at Ty, Mom, and Jackson.

They rushed in and wasted no time in closing up our circle.

But something was missing. I had to let Celine's hand fall as I reached for my phone. "I just have to check in with Tanya, Chris Babcock's old girlfriend, to see if she's coming. She was his Juliet. I think she might be the solution."

Mom looked terrified as my fingers tapped out a text. My heart pounded. Would Tanya make it here before... before what? Before he killed us all?

The cold air got even colder. I watched in horror as my friends' lips turned blue.

Celine grabbed my hand. "We have to start now."

I sucked in a breath and hoped that Tanya had received my message.

"I call on God and the angels—I ask that you protect us from danger and all that is evil. Cast your protection around us and keep us safe from all malevolent entities who wish to harm us. I ask you to send Chris on to the other side and leave this building now."

Nothing changed. In fact, if anything, the situation intensified. The wind picked up. The curtains went from an occasional flutter to flapping like a flag in a hurricane.

"Jesus." John's face reflected the shock we were all feeling.

My phone buzzed. I glanced at Celine to get permission. She nodded, and I took my phone out of my pocket.

The message from Tanya read, "Stuck in traffic on I-90 bridge."

Despite the freezing temperature, sweat prickled my forehead. If she didn't get here soon...

I jammed my phone back in my pocket, and grasped the hands of my companions again. "Stuck in traffic," I mouthed to Celine.

She shook her head. "Okay, then. We need to move to Plan B."

Benny raised his eyebrows. "We have a Plan B?"

"We need to talk him into moving on ourselves."

"Are you kidding?" Mom asked. "It doesn't seem like he wants to sit down and chat."

"It's something we need to try. You'd be surprised how many times that works." Celine motioned for everyone to drop their hands. She walked out into the space in front of the stage and turned to face the empty seats. "First you name him," she told us. "That will get his attention and he'll perhaps listen."

A low chuckling noise came from behind her.

Goosebumps erupted on my arms.

Celine turned to face the stage. "Chris Babcock. I ask you to reveal yourself to us."

A hammer that was lying in a pile with tools and other odds and ends lifted into the air and flew toward Celine. She ducked as it whizzed past her.

She righted herself and said, "Chris Babcock. You are no longer a part of the physical world. Your body died in 1984. Your spirit needs to cross over to the other side."

Another low chuckle sounded from behind the curtain. His cold, heartless laugh made my skin crawl.

"Chris," Celine repeated, "you're dead. Go to where the light is—your mother is there waiting for you."

A stool at the corner of the stage flew up into the air and was tossed at Celine. It caught her in the elbow. She staggered backward, but didn't fall.

"Do we have a Plan C?" I heard Jackson say. "I don't think this is working."

I couldn't let this happen. The ghost was going to hurt her. I ran to where she stood and linked arms with her. "Leave her alone!"

The random items on the stage—a toolbox, a measuring tape, a bucket of paint and some brushes—all lifted into the air and began to spiral like they were caught up in a tornado.

An ethereal voice came from the middle of the stage. "My Juliet. You'll finally make good on your promise."

The tornado lurched toward Celine and me. I grabbed her arm and dove under the rim of the stage as the items hit the row of seats behind us.

My phone buzzed. I fumbled in my pocket to look at the screen.

"I'm here. The door is locked," the text read.

"Miguel!" I yelled. "Tanya's at the door. Let her in!"

Miguel stood, rooted to the spot, his face frozen in terror.

"I'll do it." Benny hightailed it out of the auditorium and was back seconds later with Tanya.

She glanced around the auditorium in alarm. "What's happening?"

Celine stood up and gingerly rubbed her elbow. "It's Chris." She reached her good arm toward Tanya. "Are you able to do this? He needs to see you. We've got to get him out of this killing mode."

Tanya wrapped her arms around herself. "I… I don't see him."

"What do we do now?" I whispered to Celine.

She turned to face the stage. "Chris Babcock. Show yourself. There's someone here to see you."

The wind whipped my hair around my face. "Tanya, come here!" I shouted.

I crossed the floor quickly and took Tanya's arm to gently lead her to where Celine was standing. "You've got to do this."

Tanya's eyes reflected the fear that I felt inside. She looked like a cornered wild animal, ready to bolt at the slightest sign of danger. "What... what do I say?"

I grabbed her hand. "Tell him who you are. Ask him to show himself."

"Chris," Tanya whispered. "It's me. Can you please make yourself visible to us?"

A broom that was propped up near the exit flew across the room and hit the back of my leg.

"Stop it!" I yelled.

"*Killllll you,*" a disembodied voice hissed.

"He's a bully," I said under my breath.

The toolbox he had thrown earlier floated into the air and then flung itself at me. I whirled around, but it caught me in the back of the head.

"Ow!" I fell forward and hit the floor. I reached to touch where the toolbox had hit. I felt warm, sticky liquid. Blood.

Tanya whirled around. "Show yourself, you coward!"

The floor rumbled. I got to my knees and then tried to stand. Celine grabbed my arm and supported my weight.

Tanya stood her ground. "Leave Jenny alone," she pleaded. "She's not your Juliet. I am. It's *me*, Chris. It's Tanya. I want to see you."

The rumble died down.

"There he is." Ty pointed to the stage.

A black smoky shape began to assemble itself, and went from black, to gray, to a semi-transparent version of a person—dressed in a Romeo costume.

"Chris?" Tanya backed up.

The ghost went from being semi-transparent to fully opaque. His face was twisted in rage. "I don't know who you are, but *she*," he said, pointing at me, "is my Juliet, my Tanya, and I intend to finish what I started."

"No." Tanya took a shaky step forward. "I'm your Juliet. This is Jenny—and she has nothing to do with you. You deal with me and leave her alone."

A glimmer of doubt crossed the ghost's face. He seemed to be studying us, comparing the two.

"It's me, Chris," Tanya pleaded. "I know I look different. I'm older. You died over thirty years ago. I didn't, and I aged. I'm forty-nine years old. I have a family—three children who are grown."

The ghost's face went through a series of expressions. Confusion, denial, and finally acceptance seemed to dawn on him. Then, without warning, explosive anger. "You!" he roared. "I trusted you."

"Trusted me to what?" Tanya shook her head. "Die along with you?"

"You said you would do it." His face was furrowed in anger. "You lied," he hissed.

"I said I would because you threatened me." Tanya's voice was shrill. "You called me names… horrible names. You pushed me around. You beat me. What did you expect me to do?"

"I expected you to comply," his voice boomed.

"See? That's the problem." Tanya raised her chin. "Jenny's right. You're nothing but a bully. And you stayed here all this time holding on to your anger."

His form whooshed forward in a blur. He was now directly in front of us, towering over Tanya.

She let out a cynical laugh and pointed at him. "That's what I'm talking about. Threatening and bullying me to get your own way. You're insane. And I'm not having it."

He squinted his eyes. "Yes, you will. I'll kill you all!" He raised his arms as if to call a storm of hatred to rage against us.

"No!" Tanya shouted in his face. "You've done enough."

His laugh reverberated throughout the auditorium. "Oh, yeah. And what are you going to do about it?"

Tanya glanced at Celine and me. "I'm going to do the only thing I can do." She met his gaze. "You don't hold any power over me." Her voice shook. "Or Jenny. Or anyone else in this life. I *forgive* you. I release you. Go home, Chris."

He was stunned. The ghost shrank back from Tanya. "Forgive?"

"You heard me." She seemed to gain strength as she went on. "I forgive you. For all the terrible things you've done to me. Go to where you were supposed to go when you took your life. Your mother is there, and you had better *pray* that she forgives you too."

Chris's face sagged. It was like all the wind had been taken out of his sails. He reached toward Tanya.

She crossed her arms. "I said I forgive you, but that doesn't mean I have to *like* you."

For the first time, he seemed powerless. His form deflated and shriveled even further. Then he was gone in a puff of lukewarm air.

Tanya collapsed into a heap on the floor.

Chapter 33

The auditorium was getting warmer by the second. All the cold air had left with the ghost.

Celine and I knelt down next to Tanya, who was sobbing on the floor.

"It's going to be all right now." Celine stroked Tanya's arm. "You did well."

"I don't know where you found the strength to stand up to him," I said. "Believe me, I know how intimidating that guy could be." I shivered just thinking about all the threatening texts and physical violence he had employed to scare me.

"Is he really gone?" Tanya's face was streaked with tears.

I nodded. "He is. Thank you for coming. He would still be here if it wasn't for you—and we'd probably all be dead."

A faint smile began to brighten her face. "I really did it. I stood up to him."

"Yes, you did it." I held my hand out to her and pulled her up to her feet. "Are you going to be all right?"

Tanya wiped her face with the back of her hand. "More than all right."

My mom came over and helped Tanya out of the auditorium. The rest of us took stock of the mess Chris had made.

"Oh God." John glanced at his watch. "We open in less than two hours. How am I going to get this all cleaned up?"

"We'll help!" Jackson started picking up the scattered tools and boards. "I can be really fast when I want to be."

"Wish he felt the same way about keeping his room clean," Mom said under her breath.

***

We had the auditorium cleaned up in less than an hour. With all of us working together, it wasn't hard to get it all done in a short time.

Tanya had gone home to hopefully move on with her life. I was happy to see a spring in her step as she walked to her car.

Mom had made a run to one of the local restaurants to get us all dinner, and came back carrying bags of food. We settled on the floor of the lobby to eat before the rest of the cast arrived.

"Sorry this visit was so stressful—and dangerous." I felt terrible about ruining my friends' visit to Seattle.

Cassandra's face lit up. "No, it was awesome!"

Benny's eyebrows shot upward. "Are you kidding?"

"I mean, a typical trip to Seattle for us would entail shopping and maybe a little sightseeing." Cassandra stuffed a handful of chips in her mouth and crunched loudly. "But how many times can a girl say she got to send an evil ghost to the other side? This was the best vacation ever!"

***

I stood in the wings, waiting for my cue. Opening night was always special—you could feel the energy of the audience. Tonight was electric.

A cool breeze rustled the fabric of my dress. I froze.

Was he back?

But then a stagehand passed a prop back to an actor, and I realized that was what was causing the air to flow around me. I let out a deep sigh.

Once again, I had survived an extreme situation. Without the help of my friends, I could be dead, and Chris Babcock would still be rooted to this theatre—even when the walls came tumbling down in a few short months.

The power of compassion was immense. Tanya had overcome her fear of her ex-boyfriend after thirty long years. Without her courage, he would've destroyed me and likely others who got in his way. Tanya had put an end to the terror through just one simple act. Forgiveness.

***

The applause was deafening. A standing ovation. The show had run so smoothly despite all that had happened before the doors opened to the public.

After the questions from the audience, we gathered in the lobby.

"You were amazing!" Cassandra hugged me fiercely.

"Thank you."

One after another, my friends and family hugged me. Mike gave me the biggest hug of all, and then thrust a huge bouquet of flowers into my arms. I desperately wanted to kiss him, but I could see Ty out of the corner of my eye. I didn't want to make this anymore awkward for him.

"You were fantastic." Mike's smile warmed my heart.

I let go of Mike and turned back to my Alaskan friends. Ty gave me a quick hug and then shrank back into the crowd. I watched him strike up a conversation with Benny and Caleb near the doors to the lobby.

I felt bad for him. It was difficult for him to see me with another guy. But I was at peace with my decision to be with Mike. And I knew that Ty would find someone to love too.

Chapter 34

After we got back home, Cassandra packed up her stuff like a whirlwind. "Oh no!" She stared at the contents of her suitcase.

"What's wrong?" My heart jumped. I was still a little jittery from today's ghostbusting event and the rush of opening night.

"We forgot to go shopping! That means I have no clothes for the school year."

I looked at the time on my phone. "The mall has been closed for over an hour now. When does your flight leave tomorrow?"

"At three o'clock." She blew the hair out of her face with a haggard puff of breath. "But you'll be right in the middle of your matinee."

"I can take you in the morning. The mall opens at ten."

Her face instantly lit up in a big grin. "Awesome! And Ty too, right? He clearly needs to improve his wardrobe."

I laughed. "Of course. Maybe I'll take Benny along to be Ty's fashion consultant."

"Benny can come, but he *cannot* give Ty any clothing advice. His style is way different than Ty's."

"You're right. Benny would have Ty wearing preppy sweaters and boat shoes."

Cassandra scrunched up her face. "That wouldn't do in Sitka."

***

The next morning was cold and crisp. From my bedroom window, I watched the last leaves fall off the trees in our front yard. Winter was fast approaching, but I already yearned for the long days of summer.

Cassandra returned from the bathroom, her hair a dripping mass of curls. She toweled her hair vigorously and then raked a large brush through the tangles.

"I'm called to the theatre at one o'clock. We have exactly two and a half hours to shop." I gave Cassandra a stern look. "That means we have no time to waste."

"I can be ready in five minutes." She sat down on the floor and put on her shoes. "Except, I'll need breakfast. You know what they say… it's the most important meal of the day."

"Every meal is the most important meal of the day in your world." I grinned at her.

She took a moment to reflect. "Yeah, I think that's true. Do you think your mom made bacon?"

I rolled my eyes. "Let's go find out."

Ty was already downstairs waiting for us. Mom had made her amazing scones with raspberry jam. And sure enough, there was a big plate of bacon to go along with them.

"Yes!" Cassandra pumped her fist in the air and began piling food onto her plate.

"Coffee?" Mom held out the carafe.

"Yes, please," we all said at once.

Mom watched Cassandra gobble down at least six slices of bacon and two scones, all in the span of a few minutes. "My goodness, you sure have worked up an appetite. And yet, you're so skinny."

"Getting rid of ghosts burns a lot of calories," Cassandra managed to say in between bites.

Ty was more reserved this morning. His appetite seemed the opposite of Cassandra's. He was nibbling on a piece of bacon and hadn't even touched his scone.

"You all right?" I handed him a cup of coffee.

"I'm fine." He attempted a smile, but it quickly faded.

God, I felt bad. I'd hurt him. I needed to say something to make this all better. "Ty, can I talk to you in private?"

He looked uncomfortable, but got up from his seat.

Cassandra raised one eyebrow but didn't slow down her eating.

"Take your coffee."

He took his cup and I grabbed mine before we went out the back door.

It was chilly outside. A light dusting of frost coated the deck. I could see our breath in the morning air.

I wrapped my hands around my warm mug and took a sip of the steaming liquid. "Look, Ty." I bit my lip. "I'm so sorry you had to be around Mike yesterday. And I'm sorry that I hurt you."

He put his hand on my arm. "It's all right. I know you don't mean to hurt me. It's just that—seeing you with him. It hurts more than I thought it would, you know?"

I looked down at my shoes. "I'm so sorry."

"Don't be. You were honest. I appreciate that you told me the truth." He looked out into the backyard and to the trees beyond.

"Thank you for that. But Ty, I really don't want this to get in the way of our friendship—I don't want it hanging over us and making things awkward between us."

"Yeah. I get it." He looked back at me. "You know what really sucks?"

"What?"

"You're the perfect girl for me. We have so much in common—the healing and psychic stuff. How am I ever going to find a girl that's more perfect for me than you?"

My heart sank. "Ty…"

217

He sighed. "No, I shouldn't have said that. I don't want to make you feel worse than you already do. Jenny, if you ever change your mind about Mike, keep me in mind, would you?"

I smiled and blinked back tears. "You know if I hadn't fallen for Mike first, I would be with you, right?"

He sniffed. "That's the hard part to accept. I guess it's all in the timing."

I set my cup on the railing and hugged him. He still had that lingering scent of the ocean and the clean smell of pine. I sobbed on his shoulder.

He pulled away to look at my face. "We'll always be friends, okay? No matter what."

***

A few hours later, both Cassandra and Ty had new clothes for the school year. My friends were jammed into my car with all their luggage. I pulled up to the curb at the airport and popped the trunk.

Benny rolled out of the front seat and opened the back door for Cassandra and Ty.

They slid out and pulled the bags out of my car.

I was sad that our time together had come to an end. As we huddled together for a group hug, I couldn't help but realize that these people were my closest friends in the world—and there wasn't anything I wouldn't do for them. Would the four of us ever have the chance to hang out together again? Or would life take us in different directions? I hated to think that they would become a part of my past instead a part of my present.

As if she'd read my mind, Cassandra stuck out her little finger. "We need to make a pact. No matter where we end up for college or afterward, we meet at least once a year."

We laughed and joined our pinky fingers together.

I cleared my throat. "Who knows, maybe we'll solve a crime together—or send another naughty ghost to the other side. I feel like you guys are my family. Whenever we meet, we have awesome adventures. Thanks for being my friends."

Chapter 35

In between the matinee and evening shows, I changed in the dressing room. The chaos of girls throwing their hair into haphazard pony tails and undressing and dressing exploded all around me.

Finally, I had time to focus on the show itself, and life in the theatre. I glanced at myself in the mirror. Despite the dark circles under my eyes, I looked okay. My hair was styled in the pretty Renaissance fashion—loose curls and a few delicate braids. I reapplied hairspray and swiped some concealer under my eyes. There.

I pulled on my light down jacket and went outside the side door. Among the clusters of actors waiting to head to the restaurants downtown was Mike. My heart skipped a beat and joy filled me.

He came toward me and gave me a hug. "Thought I'd surprise you. Are you free for an early dinner?"

"Absolutely." I looked up at him, admiring his handsome face and green eyes.

Mike grabbed my hand and we walked to his car. "Where to? Bennett's?"

"Sounds great."

After we were seated, Mike scooted closer to me. "So, it seems like you're willing to give our relationship another shot. For real, right?"

I took his hand. "For real. I guess I realized that you're the one for me—at least for now."

He laughed. "Oh, for now, huh? Until you find a more suitable model?"

My face burned. "No, I didn't mean it that way. I mean, for now, I can't picture myself with anyone else. Who knows where I'll end up for college or where I'll be living. I want to just enjoy every minute I have with you."

"Then that's good enough for me." He kissed me lightly on the lips. He looked deep into my eyes. "I'm in love with you, Jenny."

Warmth radiated through me. I smiled at him and kissed him back. "I'm in love with you too, Mike."

The End

About the Author

Martina Dalton writes young adult fiction and lives in the Pacific Northwest with her family. Born and raised in Alaska, she can nimbly catch a fish, dress for rain, and know what to do when encountering a grizzly bear. Now living in the Seattle area, she uses those same skills to navigate through rush-hour traffic.

When she's not writing, she hangs out here:
https://www.facebook.com/AuthorMartinaDalton

See her website for news about author appearances, other book events, and upcoming titles:

http://www.martinadalton.com/

Other books by the author:
The Third Eye of Jenny Crumb
The Sixth Sense of Jenny Crumb

www.ingramcontent.com/pod-product-compliance
Lightning Source LLC
Chambersburg PA
CBHW060916180626
46817CB00004B/1279